CU00485242

Petals on

Ruskin Bond is known for his signature simplistic and witty writing style. He is the author of several bestselling short stories, novellas, collections, essays and children's books; and has contributed a number of poems and articles to various magazines and anthologies. At the age of twenty-three, he won the prestigious John Llewellyn Rhys Prize for his first novel, *The Room on the Roof*. He was also the recipient of the Padma Shri in 1999, Lifetime Achievement Award by the Delhi Government in 2012, and the Padma Bhushan in 2014.

Born in 1934, Ruskin Bond grew up in Jamnagar, Shimla, New Delhi and Dehradun. Apart from three years in the UK, he has spent all his life in India, and now lives in Landour, Mussoorie, with his adopted family.

RUSKIN
BOND
Petals on the Ganga

RUPA

Published by
Rupa Publications India Pvt. Ltd 2019
7/16, Ansari Road, Daryaganj
New Delhi 110002

Sales centres:
Allahabad Bengaluru Chennai
Hyderabad Jaipur Kathmandu
Kolkata Mumbai

ISBN: 978-93-5333-397-3

Second impression 2019

10 9 8 7 6 5 4 3 2

Printed at Nutech Print Services, Faridabad

CONTENTS

INTRODUCTION

There's a stream near my cottage. Cold mountain water flows down it all year round. Many a times I have sat on the rocks near it and written the odd poem, while basking in the sun.

I never cease to wonder at the tenacity of water—its ability to make its way through various strata of rock, zigzagging, backtracking, finding space, cunningly discovering faults and fissures in the mountain, and sometimes travelling underground for great distances before emerging into the open. Of course, there's no stopping water. For no matter how tiny that little trickle, it has to go somewhere!

Such streams are luxuries left only to the mountains now. And I make sure to make most of this luxury while it's still available to some of us. It was while I was living in England in the jostle and drizzle of London, that I remembered the Himalayas at their most vivid. I had grown up amongst those great blue and brown mountains, they had nourished my blood, and though I was separated from them by thousands of miles of ocean, plain and desert, I could not forget them. It is always the same with mountains. Once you have lived with them for any length of time, you belong to them. There is no escape.

This collection of my stories, which are mostly autobiographical, is based on the same theme: Nature. From the mountains that are in my blood to the trees on those very mountains for centuries and the birds that would fly into my cottage from the forests nearby to the lesser-known roads that take one to lovely winter gardens—in this book you will find descriptions of them all and much more. I shall now leave you with these stories and hope that you may find the charm of these small hill towns as irresistible as I have through all these decades.

Ruskin Bond

MOUNTAINS IN MY BLOOD

It was while I was living in England, in the jostle and drizzle of London, that I remembered the Himalayas at their most vivid. I had grown up amongst those great blue and brown mountains; they had nourished my blood; and though I was separated from them by thousands of miles of ocean, plains and desert, I could not rid them from my system. It is always the same with mountains. Once you have lived with them for any length of time, you belong to them.

And so, in London in March, the fog became a mountain mist, and the boom of traffic became the boom of the Ganges emerging from the foothills.

I remembered a little mountain path which led my restless feet into a cool, sweet forest of oak and rhododendron, and then on to the windswept crest of a naked hilltop. The hill was called Clouds End. It commanded a view of the plains on one side, and of the snow peaks on the other. Little silver rivers twisted across the valley below, where the rice-fields formed a patchwork of emerald green. And on the hill itself, the wind made a hoo-hoo-hoo in the branches of the tall deodars where it found itself trapped. During the rains, cloud enveloped the valley but left the hill alone, an island in the sky.

On a spur of the hill stood the ruins of an old brewery. The roof had long since disappeared, and the rain had beaten the stone floors smooth and yellow. Some enterprising Englishman had spent a lifetime here, making beer for his thirsty compatriots in the plains. Now, moss and ferns and maidenhair grew from the walls. In a hollow beneath a flight of worn stone steps, a wild cat had made its home. It was a beautiful grey creature, black-striped, with pale green eyes. Sometimes it watched me from the steps or the wall, but it never came near.

No one lived on the hill, except occasionally a coal-burner in a temporary grass-thatched hut. But villagers used the path, grazing their sheep and cattle on the grassy slopes. Each cow or sheep had a bell suspended from its neck, to let the shepherd boy know of its whereabouts. The boy could then lie in the sun and eat wild strawberries without fear of losing his animals.

I remembered some of the shepherd boys and girls. There was a boy who played a flute. Its rough, sweet and straightforward notes travelled clearly across the mountain air. He would greet me with a nod of his head, without taking the flute from his lips. There was a girl who was nearly always cutting grass for fodder. She wore heavy bangles on her feet, and long silver earrings. She did not speak much either, but she always had a wide grin on her face when she met me on the path. She used to sing to herself, or to the sheep, to the grass, or to the sickle in her hand. These things I remembered—these, and the smell of pine needles, the silver of oak leaves and the red of maple, the call of the Himalayan cuckoo, and the mist, like a wet face-cloth, pressing against the hills. Odd, how some little incident, some snatch of conversation, comes back to one again and again, in the most unlikely places. Standing in the aisle of a crowded tube train on a Monday morning, my nose tucked into the back page of someone else's newspaper, I suddenly had a vision of a bear making off with a ripe pumpkin.

A bear and a pumpkin—and there, between Goodge Street and Tottenham Court Road stations, all the smells and sounds of the Himalayas came rushing back to me.

THE LAST WALNUT

It was nice to have a walnut tree just outside the window. It was a tree for all seasons. In winter, the branches were bare; but they were smooth, straight and round like the arms of an apsara. In spring, each branch produced a hard bright spear of new leaf. By midsummer the entire tree was in leaf, and towards the end of the monsoon the walnuts, encased in their green jackets, had reached their full maturity.

Then the jackets began to split, revealing the hard brown shell of the walnuts. Inside the shell was the nut itself. Look closely at the nut, and you will notice that it is shaped rather like the human brain. No wonder the ancients prescribed walnuts for headaches.

Every year the tree made us a gift of a basket of walnuts. But last year the walnuts were disappearing one by one, and I was at a loss to know who had been taking them.

Could it have been Bijju, the milkman's son? He was an inveterate tree-climber. But he was usually found up oak trees, gathering fodder for his cows. He told me that the cows did not care for walnuts. He admitted that they had relished my dahlias which they had eaten the previous week, but he denied having given them any walnuts.

Later, I found a fat langur sitting in the walnut tree. I watched him for some time to see if he was going to help himself to the nuts, but he was only sunning himself. When he thought I wasn't looking, he came down and ate the geraniums; but he did not take any walnuts.

It wasn't the woodpecker. He was out there every day, knocking furiously against the bark of the tree, trying to prise an insect out of a narrow crack. He was strictly non-vegetarian and none the worse for it.

The walnuts had been disappearing early in the morning, while I was still in bed. So one morning I surprised everyone, including myself, by getting up before sunrise. I was just in time to catch the culprit climbing down the walnut tree.

She was an old woman, who sometimes came to cut grass on the hillside. Her face was as wrinkled as the walnuts she had been pinching. But in spite of her age, her arms and legs were sturdy. When she saw me, she was as swift as a civet cat in getting out of the tree.

'Only two,' she said with a giggle, offering them to me on her outstretched palm.

I took one of the walnuts; and thus encouraged, she climbed back into the tree and helped herself to the remaining walnuts. It was impossible to object. I was taken up in admiring her agility in the tree, and wondering if I could ever do the same.

Last winter the PWD decided to take a new road past my doorstep, and the first casualty was the walnut tree. Along with a large number of different trees growing below the cottage, it fell to the contractors' axes.

Recently when I met the old woman on the road, I asked

her, 'Where do you get your walnuts now, Grandmother?'

'Nowhere,' she answered stoically. 'That was the last walnut tree on the hillside.'

THE VANISHING TREES

The peace and quiet of the Maplewood hillside disappeared forever one winter. The powers that be decided to build another new road into the mountains and the PWD saw fit to take it right past the cottage, about six feet from the window which overlooked the forest.

In my journal, I wrote: Already they have felled most of the trees. The walnut was one of the first to go. A tree I had lived with for over ten years, watching it grow as I had watched Prem's young son Rakesh grow up, looking forward to its new leaf-buds, the broad green leaves of summer turning to spears of gold in September when the walnuts were ripe and ready to fall. I knew this tree better than the others. It was just below the window where a buttress for the road is going up.

Another tree I will miss is the young deodar, the only one growing in this stretch of the woods. Some years ago it was stunted due to lack of sunlight. The oaks covered it with their shaggy branches, so I cut away some of the overhanging ones and after that the deodar grew much faster. It was just coming into its own this year—now cut down in its prime, like my young brother on the road to Delhi last month. Both victims of the road—the tree killed by the PWD, my brother by a truck.

Twenty oaks have been felled just in this small stretch near the cottage. By the time this bypass reaches Jabarkhet, about six miles from here, over a thousand oaks will have been slaughtered, besides many other fine trees—maples, deodars and pines—most of them unnecessary as they grew some fifty or sixty yards from the roadside.

The trouble is, hardly anyone (with the exception of the contractor who buys the felled trees) really believes that trees and shrubs are necessary. They get in the way so much, don't they? According to my milkman, the only useful tree is the one which can be picked clean of its leaves for fodder! Another young man remarked to me, 'You should come to Pauri. The view is terrific, there's not a tree on the way!'

Well, he can stay here now and enjoy the ravaged hillside. But as the oaks have gone, the milkman will have to look further afield for his fodder.

Rakesh calls the maples 'butterfly trees' because when the winged seeds fall, they flutter like butterflies in the breeze. No maples now. No bright red leaves to flame against the sky. No birds! That is to say, no birds near the house. No longer will it be possible for me to open the window and watch the scarlet minivets flitting through the dark green foliage of the oaks the long tailed magpies gliding through the trees, the barbet calling insistently from his perch on the top of the deodar.

Forest birds, all of them, they will now be in search of some other stretch of surviving forests. The only visitors will be the crows who have learnt to live with and off humans, and seem to multiply along with roads, houses and people. And even when all the people have gone, the crows will still be there.

Other things to look forward to—trucks thundering past in

the night, perhaps a tea and pakora shop around the corner. The grinding of gears, the music of motor horns. Will the whistling thrush be heard above them? The explosions that continually shatter the silence of the mountains as thousand-year-old rocks are dynamited, have frightened away all but the most intrepid of birds and animals. Even the bold langurs haven't shown their faces for over a fortnight.

Somehow, I don't think we shall wait for the tea shop to arrive. There must be some other quiet corner, possibly on the next mountain where new roads have yet to come into being. No doubt this is a negative attitude and if I have any sense I'd open my own tea shop. To retreat is to be a loser. But the trees are losers too but when they fall, they do so with a certain dignity.

Never mind. Men come and go, the mountains remain.

THE TENACITY OF MOUNTAIN WATER

Early in the summer the grass on the hills is still a pale yellowish green, tinged with brown, and that is how it remains until the monsoon rains bring new life to everything that subsists on the stony Himalayan soil. And then, for four months, the greens are deep and dark and emerald bright.

But the other day, taking a narrow path that left the dry Mussoorie ridge to link up with Pari Tibba (Fairy Hill), I ran across a patch of lush green grass, and I knew there had to be water there.

The grass was soft and springy, spotted with the crimson of small, wild strawberries. Delicate maidenhair, my favorite fern, grew from a cluster of moist, glistening rocks. Moving the ferns a little, I discovered the spring, a freshet of clear sparkling water.

I never cease to wonder at the tenacity of water—its ability to make its way through various strata of rock, zigzagging, backtracking, finding space, cunningly discovering faults and fissures in the mountain, and sometimes travelling underground for great distances before emerging into the open. Of course, there's no stopping water. For no matter how tiny that little trickle, it has to go somewhere!

Like this little spring. At first I thought it was too small to go anywhere... That it would dry up at the edge of the path. Then I discovered that the grass remained soft and green for some distance along the verge, and that there was moisture beneath the grass. This wet stretch ended abruptly; but, on looking further, I saw that it continued on the other side of the path, after briefly going underground again.

I decided to follow its fortunes as it disappeared beneath a tunnel of tall grass and bracken fern. Slithering down a stony slope, I found myself in a small ravine, and there I discovered that my little spring had grown, having been joined by the waters of another spring bubbling up from beneath a patch of primroses.

A short distance away, a spotted forktail stood on a rock, surveying this marriage of the waters. His long, forked tail moved slowly up and down. He paid no attention to me, being totally absorbed in the movements of a water spider. A swift peck, and the spider vanished, completing the bird's breakfast. Thirsty, I cupped my hands and drank a little water. So did the forktail. We had a perennial supply of pure *aqua minerale* all to ourselves!

There was now a rivulet to follow, and I continued down the ravine until I came to a small pool that was fed not only by my brook (I was already thinking of it as my very own!) but also by a little cascade of water coming down from a rocky ledge. I climbed a little way up the rocks and entered a small cave, in which there was just enough space for crouching down. Water dripped and trickled off its roof and sides. And most wonderful of all, some of these drops created tiny rainbows, for a ray of sunlight had struck through a crevice in the cave roof making the droplets of moisture radiant with all the colours of the spectrum.

When I emerged from the cave, I saw a pair of pine martens drinking at the pool. As soon as they saw me, they were up and away, bounding across the ravine and into the trees.

The brook was now a small stream, but I could not follow it much farther, because the hill went into a steep decline and the water tumbled over large, slippery boulders, becoming a waterfall and then a noisy little torrent as it sped towards the valley.

Climbing up the sides of the ravine to the spur of Pari Tibba, I could see the distant silver of a meandering river, and I knew my little stream was destined to become part of it; and that the river would be joined by another that could be seen slipping over the far horizon, and that their combined waters would enter the great Ganga, or Ganges, further downstream.

This mighty river would, in turn, wander over the rich alluvial plains of northern India, finally debouching into the ocean near the Bay of Bengal.

And the ocean, what was it but another droplet in the universe in the greater scheme of things? No greater than the glistening drop of water that helped start it all, where the grass grows greener around my little spring on the mountain.

THE TREES ARE MY BROTHERS

It's good to know that my old friend the jackfruit is finally coming into its own. Apparently it is now much in demand in the West, a fashionable substitute for meat, being used as filling for burgers, sandwiches, pies etc., with one enthusiast even calling it 'mutton hanging from a tree'.

Here in India we have always appreciated a good jackfruit curry, or even better, a jackfruit pickle. I'm a pickle friend myself, and among the twenty different pickles on my sideboard there is always a jar of jackfruit piddle; that's why I call it an old friend. But I had no idea it tasted like mutton. The seed and the pulp have their own individual flavor. As it grows on a tree we call it a fruit, but we cook it as though it were a vegetable. And it, to some, tastes like mutton, then perhaps some meat-eaters will become vegetarians. On the other hand, some vegetarians might not care for its meaty flavour!

When I was a boy, we had an old jackfruit tree growing beside the side verandah. I spent a lot of time in the trees surrounding my grandmother's bungalow, and this one was easy to climb. The others included several guava and lichi trees, lemons and grapefruits, and of course a couple of mango trees—

but these last were difficult to climb.

'Why do you spend so much time in the trees?' complained my grandmother. 'Why not do something useful for a change?'

'The trees are my brothers,' I would say, 'I like to play with them.'

And I still think of them as my brothers, although I can no longer climb trees or play in them. But I still think of them as human beings possessed of individuality and charm. Just as no two humans are exactly alike (unless they happen to be twins), so no two trees are the same. Like humans they grow from seed. They develop branches as arms and leaves like flowing hair. We give birth to children, they give birth to fruits and flowers. We shelter our young, they shelter the small creatures of the forest.

However, unlike us they spring from the soul, from the land—that very land that gives us food and pasture and protection; the land that we so casually take for granted, preferring to build upon it rather than grow upon it. Where will our cattle graze when the last green spaces have gone?

'No problem,' says a young friend. 'We can always import our milk.'

The other day I came across an old book that had been on my shelf for many years. *Farmer's Glory* by A.G. Street, written several decades ago. In his epilogue he writes:

> It is perhaps nothing to boast about, but there is little doubt that the present prosperity of British farming is mainly due to one man, who is now dead. His name was Adolf Hitler. There is no disputing that it was the fear of famine during the early 1940s which taught the British nation that despite all man's cleverness and inventions, when real danger comes an island people must turn for succour to the only permanent asset they possess, the land

of their own country. It has never, and will never, let them down; always provided they realize and obey this eternal truth—that to make the land serve man, man must first be content to serve the land.

Surely it is this love of the land and willingness to serve it that is at the heart of true patriotism. The patriotic songs and speeches that we hear from time to time are fine for stirring up the emotions, but it is really the connect between ourselves and the *'do bigha zameen'* on which we grow our fruit and grain that emboldens us to protect it.

I think I am correct in saying that most of our jawans, the young men who join the solid ranks of the Indian Army, come from rural backgrounds; some from the hills, some from the vast plains and hinterland of our country. They know the value of the land. They have grown up in villages and have worked with their families in the rice fields, or sugarcane plantations, or mango-groves, or wheat or corn or mustard or fields of an infinite variety of crops. More than city folk, they know the value of the land—its true worth in terms of either prosperity or poverty. And so they are ready to defend it, to fight for it against all corners. The best soldiers come from the soil that they and their forefathers have tilled.

So let us protect the land—not just from the intruder or the enemy, but also from those who would turn the field or the forest into one more concrete jungle.

Of course there are those who prefer concrete jungles. Like my young friend who wants to live in a Smart City and never mind the cities that are no longer smart. My advice to him (unheeded of course) is to go back to his roots, create a smart little village, and plant jackfruit trees!

PETALS ON THE GANGA

Flowers floating down the river: yellow and scarlet canna lilies, roses, jasmine and hibiscus. They are placed in boats made of broad leaves, then consigned to the water with a prayer. The current carries them swiftly downstream, and they bob about on the water for fifty, sometimes a hundred yards, before being submerged in the river. The Ganga or Ganges issues through a gorge in the mountains with a low booming sound, rushing past the town of Haridwar (Door of Lord Hari, or Vishnu), one of the most sacred of Hindu pilgrim centres.

The river is fast and muddy but this does not deter thousands of people from descending the steps to the bathing-ghats, and plunging into the cold, snow-fed water. For the Ganga is reputed to wash away all sin. Hindu mythology tells us that the Ganga descended straight from heaven. For a thousand years a devout prince stood with his arms upraised, praying for water to enable him to make the funeral obligations for the ashes of his 60,000 grand-uncles. Almost all the gods were involved in the affair. Finally, when the waters of the Ganga were released from heaven, and the river reached the earth, the Prince mounted his chariot and rode towards the spot where the ashes of his kinsmen lay. Wherever he went, the Ganga meekly followed. Gods, nymphs, demons, giants, sages and great snakes all joined the procession, and as the river hurried on, in the footsteps of the Prince, the whole multitude of created beings bathed in her sacred waters and washed away their sins.

The multitude that followed the Prince could be the same multitude that throngs the riverfront today. I see no one who is not delighted at entering the water. It is a big crowd, although this is just an ordinary day of the week and not an occasion of any religious significance. But for the Hindu every day is a good day for bathing in the Ganga.

At the time of major festivals, such as Baisakhi, which takes place at the commencement of the Hindu solar year (March–April), elaborate arrangements have to be made for the benefit of the great influx of pilgrims who come here from all corners of the country. The number of pilgrims at the Baisakhi festival usually exceeds 100,000. During the Kumbh festival, held every twelve years (when the planet Jupiter is in Aquarius and the sun enters Aries), there may be more than 500,000 present on the great bathing day. This is five times the normal population of Haridwar. And when one realizes that the town is bounded by steep hills on one side, and the river on the other, and has just the one main street leading to the riverfront, the press of people can well be imagined.

Fortunately, the main street is a broad one. I find the road shaded by tall, old peepul and banyan trees. In some places the trees reach right across the street to touch the roots of the tall, old buildings on the other side. At several places, we find young peepul trees growing out of the walls of houses. No one fells the sacred peepul. It is better that a wall should crumble! In a world where trees and forests are rapidly disappearing, this is one tree that will survive, for peepul trees are believed to be the abodes of the spirits and the man who cuts so much as a branch will be pursued by all the demons he has disturbed.

Peepuls will live for hundreds of years, and Haridwar's oldest trees must have been here long before the present town reached maturity. Some will be as old as the eleventh century Mayaduri temple, which is probably the oldest temple in Haridwar. On a sultry day, there can no spot more pleasant than the shade of a peepul tree. It is no wonder that the man who plants one of these trees is pleased by generations of Hindus to come. While I stand beneath a peepul, a devout and elderly man approaches with a watering-can, and circling the tree, waters the soil around the base of the tree trunk. I move out of the way of his sprinkler, watching the ritual with some surprise. It has been raining steadily for some days, and the trees had no need for water.

'Why do you water the tree?' I ask.

'Why does one water anything?' asks the man. 'So that it may grow and flourish, of course.'

'But it's been raining almost every day for the past week.'

'Ah, but rain is something else,' he says, 'I am not responsible for the rain. This rain is from the Ganga. It makes a lot of difference.'

I do not argue with him. He waters the tree with love and his love for the tree, as much as rain-water or river-water, is what makes it flourish.

Leaving the main street, I enter the bazaar.

The Haridwar bazaar is a long, narrow winding street, probably the oldest part of the town and free of all vehicular traffic. The road is no more than four yards wide. The smaller shops are spilling over with sweets, pickles, bead necklaces, sacred texts, ritual designs, festival images and bazaar pictures of the gods and gurus in vibrant technicolour. There is something in these naive, gaudy prints that acts as a transformer, making the more abstract philosophies of Hinduism comprehensible to anxious farmers or tired truck drivers.

The bazaar winds and turns back upon itself, and eventually I find myself back at the riverfront, gazing out across the river at the forested foothills. Few of the pilgrims on the bathing-steps can realize that sometimes at night tigers stand on the opposite bank watching the bright illuminations of the temples, or that wild elephants stand listening to the rumbling of the trains bringing pilgrims to Haridwar from all parts of India.

It is evening now, and there are fewer people at the ghats. There is a breeze coming up the river. More flowers are being sold and now the leaf-boats are lit by diyas, wicks dipped in oil. The little boats are swept away, sometimes travelling a considerable distance before being upset by submerged rocks or inquisitive fish. I, too, send an offering downstream, but my boat sails beneath the legs of a late bather, and disappears beneath the pilgrim.

WILD FLOWERS NEAR A MOUNTAIN STREAM

Below my house is a forest of oak and maple and Himalayan rhododendron. A path twists its way down through the trees, over an open ridge where red sorrel grows wild, and then steeply down through a tangle of thorn bushes, vines and rangal bamboo. At the bottom of the hill the path leads on to a grassy verge, surrounded by wild rose. A stream runs close by the verge, tumbling over smooth pebbles, over rocks worn yellow with age, on its way to the plains and the little Song River and finally to the sacred Ganges.

When I first discovered the stream it was April and the wild roses were flowering, small white blossoms lying in clusters. There were primroses on the hill slopes, and an occasional late-flowering rhododendron provided a splash of red against the dark green of the hill.

The St John's Wort was flowering profusely on small shrubs.

Many legends have grown around this flower of pure dazzling sunshine which takes its family name—Hypericaceae—from the great Titan god Hyperion, who was the father of the Greek God of the sun, Apollo.

Is a friend of yours insane? Then get him to drink the sap from the leaves and stalks of the St John's Wort. He will be well again.

Are you hurt? If your wounds do not heal, take the juice and put it on the wound; and if the bleeding will not stop, take more juice.

Is your father bald? Then he must rise early one morning and bathe his head with the dew from St John's Wort, and his hair will grow again.

Do you live on the Isle of Man? Then beware! Tread not on the St John's Wort after sunset, lest a fairy horseman arise and carry you off. He will land you anywhere.

These are all English or Irish superstitions, but the St John's Wort is as profuse in the lower ranges of the Himalayas as it is anywhere in Europe.

A spotted forktail, a bird of the Himalayan streams, was much in evidence during those early visits. It moved nimbly over the boulders with a fairy tread, and continually wagged its tail.

In May and June, when the hills are always brown and dry, it remained cool and green near the stream, where ferns and maidenhair and long grasses continued to thrive. Downstream I found a cave with water dripping from the roof, the water spangled gold and silver in the shafts of sunlight that pushed through the slits in the cave roof. Few people came there. Sometimes a milkman or a coal-burner would cross the stream on his way to a village; but the nearby hill station's summer visitors had not discovered this haven of wild and green things.

The monkeys—langurs, with white and silver-grey fur, black faces and long swishing tails—had discovered the place, but they kept to the trees and sunlit slopes. They grew quite accustomed to my presence, and carried on with their work and play as though I did not exist. The young ones scuffled and wrestled like boys, while their parents attended to each other's toilets, stretching themselves out on the grass, beautiful animals with slim waists and long sinewy legs, and tails full of character. They were clean and polite, much nicer than the red monkeys of the plains.

During the rains the stream became a rushing torrent, bushes and small trees were swept away, and the friendly murmur of the water became a threatening boom. I did not visit the spot very often. There were leeches in the long grass, and they would fasten themselves on to my legs and feast on my blood. But it was always worthwhile tramping through the forest to feast my eyes on the foliage that sprang up in tropical profusion—soft, spongy moss; great stag ferns on the trunks of trees; mysterious and sometimes evil-looking orchids; the climbing convolvulus opening its purple secrets to the morning sun; and the wood sorrel, or oxalis—so named because of the oxalic acid derived from its roots—with its clover-like leaflets, which fold down like umbrellas at the first sign of rain.

And then, after a November hailstorm, it was winter, and one could not lie on the frostbitten grass. The sound of the stream was the same, but I missed the birds.

It snowed—the snow lay heavy on the branches of the oak trees and piled up in the culverts—and the grass and the ferns and wild flowers were pressed to sleep beneath a cold white blanket; but the stream flowed on, pushing its way through and under the whiteness, towards another river, towards another spring.

GRAN'S KITCHEN

As kitchens went, it wasn't very big. What made it fabulous was all that came out of it. Gran's curries and kebabs, chocolate fudge and peanut toffee, jellies and gulab jamuns, meat pies and apple pies, stuffed chickens, stuffed eggplants, and even ham, stuffed with stuffed chicken! As far as I was concerned, Gran was the best cook in the world.

The town we lived in was called Dehradun. It's still there, though much bigger and more populous since India's independence. Gran had a large, rambling bungalow on the outskirts of town. On the grounds were many fruit trees— mangoes, lichees, guavas, bananas, papayas and lemons—there was room for all of them, including a giant jackfruit tree that threw its shadow on the walls of the house.

Gran had a saying,

'Blessed is the house upon whose walls

The shade of an old tree softly falls.'

She was right, hers was a good house to live in, especially for a ten-year-old boy with a tremendous appetite.

Every winter, when I came home from boarding school, I would spend at least a month with Gran before going over to my parents in Assam. My father managed a tea plantation there, and although the tea gardens were fun to play in, my parents couldn't cook. Like most colonials, they employed a Khansama, a professional cook, who made good mutton curry but little else. So I was always glad to spend half my holidays with Gran.

Gran was glad to have me too, because she lived alone most of the time. Not entirely alone, though. The gardener, his son Mohan and a mongrel dog named Crazy all lived in the compound. And sometimes there was Uncle Ken, a nephew of Gran's, who came to stay whenever he was out of a job (which was fairly often), or when he felt like enjoying some of Gran's cooking.

Gran didn't enjoy cooking just for herself; she liked to have someone to cook for. And although Uncle Ken sometimes appreciated her efforts, and Crazy loved her table scraps, a good cook likes a kid to feed, because kids are adventurous and ready to try even the most unusual dishes.

Whenever Gran tried out a new recipe on me, she would wait for my reaction, and then jot down some of my comments in a notebook. This was useful when she wanted to try the same dish on others.

'Do you like it?' she'd ask, after I'd taken a few mouthfuls.

'Yes, Gran.'

'Sweet enough?'

'Yes, Gran.'

'Not *too* sweet?'

'No, Gran.'

'Would you like some more?'

'Yes please, Gran.'

'Well, finish it off.'

'Mmmm…'

'Eat well, but don't overeat,' Gran used to tell me. And we did eat well, even though all those wonderful meals consisted of only one course followed by a sweet dish. It was Gran's cooking that turned a modest meal into a feast.

Roast duck was one of her specialties. The first time I had roast duck at Gran's place, Uncle Ken was there too. He'd just lost his job as a railway guard, and had come to stay with Gran until he could find something else.

Uncle Ken ate just as much as I did, but he never praised Gran's dishes and that annoyed me. He looked at the roast duck, his glasses slipping down to the edge of his nose. 'Hmmm... Duck again, Aunt May?'

'What do you mean by duck *again*? We haven't had duck since you were here last month!'

'That's what I mean,' said Uncle Ken. 'Somehow, one expects a little more variety.'

All the same, he took two large helpings and ate most of the stuffing before I could get at it. I got my revenge by emptying all the applesauce onto my plate. Uncle Ken knew I loved stuffing, and I knew he was crazy about Gran's applesauce. So we were even.

Gran was famous all over Dehra for her pickles. Green mangoes, pickled in oil, were always popular. So was her hot lime pickle. And she was adept at pickling turnips, carrots, cauliflowers, and chillies. She could pickle almost any fruit or vegetable—everything from nasturtium seeds to jackfruit.

One winter, when Gran's funds were low, Mohan and I went from house to house...selling pickles for her. Major Clarke, our neighbour across the road, was our first customer.

'And what have you got there?' he asked.

'Pickles, sir.'

'Pickles? Did you make them?'

'No, sir, they're my grandmother's. We're selling them so we can buy a turkey for Christmas.'

'Mrs Bond's pickles, eh? Well, I'm glad this is the first house on your route, because that basket will soon be empty. There's no one who can make a pickle like your grandmother! What have you this time? Stuffed chillies, I hope. She knows they're my favorite. I shall be deeply wounded if there are no stuffed chillies in that basket.'

There were, in fact, three bottles of stuffed red chillies in the basket, and Major Clarke bought all of them.

Further down the road, Dr Dutt bought several bottles of lime pickle, saying it was good for his liver. And Mr Hari, who owned a garage at the end of the road, purchased two bottles of pickled onions and begged us to bring another as soon as we could.

By the time we got home, the basket was empty, and Gran was richer by thirty rupees—enough, in those days, for a turkey.

Uncle Ken stayed for Christmas and ate most of the turkey.

THE JOY OF WATER

Each drop represents a little bit of creation—and of life itself. When the monsoon brings to northern India the first rains of summer, the parched earth opens its pores and quenches its thirst with a hiss of ecstasy. After baking in the sun for the last few months, the land looks cracked, dusty and tired. Now, almost overnight, new grass springs up, there is renewal everywhere, and the damp earth releases a fragrance sweeter than any devised by man.

Water brings joy to earth, grass, leaf-bud, blossom, insect, bird, animal and the pounding heart of man. Small children run out of their homes to romp naked in the rain. Buffaloes, which have spent the summer listlessly around lakes gone dry, now plunge into a heaven of muddy water. Soon the lakes and rivers will overflow with the monsoon's generosity. Trekking in the Himalayan foothills, I recently walked for kilometres without encountering habitation. I was just scolding myself for not having brought along a water bottle, when I came across a patch of green on a rock face. I parted a curtain of tender maidenhair fern and discovered a tiny spring issuing from the rock-nectar for the thirsty traveller.

I stayed there for hours, watching the water descend, drop by drop, into a tiny casement in the rocks. Each drop reflected creation. That same spring, I later discovered, joined other springs to form a swift, tumbling stream, which went cascading down the hill into other streams until, in the plains, it became part of a river. And that river flowed into another mightier river that kilometres later emptied into the ocean. Be like water, taught Lao-tzu, philosopher and founder of Taoism. Soft and limpid, it finds its way through, over or under any obstacle. It does not quarrel; it simply moves on.

A small pool in the rocks outside my cottage in the Mussoorie hills, provides me endless delight. Water beetles paddle the surface, while tiny fish lurk in the shallows. Sometimes a spotted forktail comes to drink, hopping delicately from rock to rock. And once I saw a barking deer, head lowered at the edge of the pool. I stood very still, anxious that it should drink its fill. It did, and then, looking up, saw me and leapt across the ravine to disappear into the forest.

In summer the pool is almost dry. Even this morning, there was just enough water for the fish and tadpoles to survive. But as I write, there is a pattering on the tin roof of the cottage, and I look out to see the raindrops pitting the surface of the pool.

Tomorrow the spotted forktail will be back. Perhaps the barking deer will return. I open the window wide and allow the fragrance of the rain and freshened earth to waft into my room.

SOUNDS I LIKE TO HEAR

All night the rain has been drumming on the corrugated tin roof. There has been no storm, no thunder just the steady swish of a tropical downpour. It helps one to lie awake; at the same time, it doesn't keep one from sleeping.

It is a good sound to read by the rain outside, the quiet within—and, although tin roofs are given to springing unaccountable leaks, there is in general a feeling of being untouched by, and yet in touch with, the rain.

Gentle rain on a tin roof is one of my favourite sounds. And early in the morning, when the rain has stopped, there are other sounds I like to hear—a crow shaking the raindrops from his feathers and cawing rather disconsolately; babblers and bulbuls bustling in and out of bushes and long grass in search of worms and insects; the sweet, ascending trill of the Himalayan whistling-thrush; dogs rushing through damp undergrowth.

A cherry tree, bowed down by the heavy rain, suddenly rights itself, flinging pellets of water in my face.

Some of the best sounds are made by water. The water of a mountain stream, always in a hurry, bubbling over rocks and chattering, 'I'm late, I'm late!' like the White Rabbit, tumbling over itself in its anxiety to reach the bottom of the hill, the sound of the sea, especially when it is far away—or when you hear it by putting a sea shell to your ear. The sound made by dry and thirsty earth, as it sucks at a sprinkling of water. Or the sound of a child drinking thirstily the water running down his chin and throat.

Water gushing out of the pans of an old well outside a village while a camel moves silently round the well. Bullock-cart wheels creaking over rough country roads. The clip-clop of a pony carriage, and the tinkle of its bell, and the singsong call of its driver...

Bells in the hills. A schoolbell ringing, and children's voices drifting through an open window. A temple-bell, heard faintly from across the valley. Heavy silver ankle-bells on the feet of sturdy hill women. Sheep bells heard high up on the mountainside.

Do falling petals make a sound? Just the tiniest and softest of sounds, like the drift of falling snow. Of course big flowers, like dahlias, drop their petals with a very definite flop. These are showoffs, like the hawk-moth who comes flapping into the rooms at night instead of emulating the butterfly dipping lazily on the afternoon breeze.

One must return to the birds for favourite sounds, and the birds of the plains differ from the birds of the hills. On a cold winter morning in the plains of northern India, if you walk some way into the jungle you will hear the familiar call of the black partridge: *Bhagwan teri giedrat* it seems to cry, which means: 'Oh God! Great is thy might.'

The cry rises from the bushes in all directions; but an hour later not a bird is to be seen or heard and the jungle is so very still that the silence seems to shout at you.

There are sounds that come from a distance, beautiful because they are far away, voices on the wind—they 'walketh upon the wings of the wind'. The cries of fishermen out on the river. Drums beating rhythmically in a distant village. The croaking of frogs from the rainwater pond behind the house. I mean frogs at a distance. A frog croaking beneath one's window is as welcome as a motor horn.

But some people like motor horns. I know a taxi-driver who never misses an opportunity to use his horn. It was made to his own specifications, and it gives out a resonant bugle-call. He never tires of using it. Cyclists and pedestrians always scatter at his approach. Other cars veer off the road. He is proud of his horn. He loves its strident sound, which only goes to show that some men's sounds are other men's noises!

Homely sounds, though we don't often think about them, are the ones we miss most when they are gone. A kettle on the boil. A door that creaks on its hinges. Old sofa springs. Familiar voices lighting up the dark. Ducks quacking in the rain.

And so we return to the rain, with which my favourite sounds began.

I have sat out in the open at night, after a shower of rain when the whole air is murmuring and tinkling with the voices of crickets and grasshoppers and little frogs. There is one melodious sound, a sweet repeated trill, which I have never been able to trace to its source. Perhaps it is a little tree frog. Or it may be a small green cricket. I shall never know.

I am not sure that I really want to know. In an age when a scientific and rational explanation has been given for almost everything we see and touch and hear, it is good to be left with one small mystery, a mystery sweet and satisfying and entirely my own.

Listen!

Listen to the night wind in the trees,
Listen to the summer grass singing;
Listen to the time that's tripping by,
And the dawn dew falling.
Listen to the moon as it climbs the sky,
Listen to the pebbles humming;
Listen to the mist in the trembling leaves,
And the silence calling.

GUESTS WHO FLY IN FROM THE FOREST

When mist fills the Himalayan valleys, and heavy monsoon rain sweeps across the hills, it is natural for wild creatures to seek shelter. Any shelter is welcome in a storm—and sometimes my cottage in the forest is the most convenient refuge.

There is no doubt that I make things easier for all concerned by leaving most of my windows open—I am one of those peculiar people who like to have plenty of fresh air indoors—and if a few birds, beasts and insects come in too, they're welcome, provided they don't make too much of a nuisance of themselves.

I must confess that I did lose patience with a bamboo beetle who blundered in the other night and fell into the water jug. I rescued him and pushed him out of the window. A few seconds later he came whirring in again, and with unerring accuracy landed with a plop in the same jug. I fished him out once more and offered him the freedom of the night. But attracted no doubt by the light and warmth of my small sitting-room, he came buzzing back, circling the room like a helicopter looking for a good place to land. Quickly I covered the water jug. He landed in a bowl of wild dahlias, and I allowed him to remain there, comfortably curled up in the hollow of a flower.

Sometimes, during the day, a bird visits me—a deep purple whistling-thrush, hopping about on long dainty legs, peering to right and left, too nervous to sing. She perches on the windowsill, looking out at the rain. She does not permit any familiarity. But if I sit quietly in my chair, she will sit quietly on her windowsill, glancing quickly at me now and then just to make sure that I'm keeping my distance. When the rain stops, she glides away, and it is only then, confident in her freedom, that she bursts into full-throated song, her broken but haunting melody echoing down the ravine.

A squirrel comes sometimes, when his home in the oak tree gets waterlogged. Apparently he is a bachelor; anyway, he lives alone. He knows me well, this squirrel, and is bold enough to climb on to the dining-table looking for tidbits which he always finds, because I leave them there deliberately. Had I met him when he was a youngster, he would have learned to eat from my hand; but I have only been here a few months. I like it this way. I am not looking for pets: these are simply guests.

Last week, as I was sitting down at my desk to write a long-deferred article, I was startled to see an emerald-green praying mantis sitting on my writing pad. He peered up at me with his protruberant glass bead eyes, and I stared down at him through my reading glasses. When I gave him a prod, he moved off in a leisurely way. Later I found him examining the binding of Whitman's *Leaves of Grass;* perhaps he had found a succulent bookworm. He disappeared for a couple of days, and then I found him on the dressing-table, preening himself before the mirror. Perhaps I am doing him an injustice in assuming that he was preening. Maybe he thought he'd met another mantis and was simply trying to make contact. Anyway, he seemed fascinated by his reflection.

Out in the garden, I spotted another mantis, perched on the jasmine bush. Its arms were raised like a boxer's. Perhaps they're a pair, I thought, and went indoors and fetched my mantis and placed him on the jasmine bush, opposite his fellow insect. He did not like what he saw—no comparison with his own image!—and made off in a huff.

My most interesting visitor comes at night, when the lights are still burning—a tiny bat who prefers to fly in at the door, should it be open, and will use the window only if there's no alternative. His object in entering the house is to snap up the moths that cluster around the lamps.

All the bats I've seen fly fairly high, keeping near the ceiling as far as possible, and only descending to ear level (my ear level) when they must; but this particular bat flies in low, like a dive bomber, and does acrobatics amongst the furniture, zooming in and out of chair legs and under tables. Once, while careening about the room in this fashion, he passed straight between my legs.

Has his radar gone wrong, I wondered, or is he just plain crazy?

I went to my shelves of *Natural History* and looked up Bats, but could find no explanation for this erratic behaviour. As a last resort, I turned to an ancient volume, Sterndale's *Indian Mammalia* (Calcutta, 1884), and in it, to my delight, I found what I was looking for:

> …a bat found near Mussoorie by Captain Hutton, on the southern range of hills at 5,500 feet; head and body, 1.4 inch; skims close to the ground, instead of flying high as bats generally do, Habitat, Jharipani, N.W. Himalayas.

Apparently the bat was rare even in 1884.

Perhaps I've come across one of the few surviving members of the species: Jharipani is only two miles from where I live. And I feel rather offended that modern authorities should have ignored this tiny bat; possibly they feel that it is already extinct. If so, I'm pleased to have rediscovered it. I am happy that it survives in my small corner of the woods, and I undertake to celebrate it in prose and verse.

IN SEARCH OF A WINTER GARDEN

If someone were to ask me to choose between writing an essay on the Taj Mahal or on the last rose of summer, I'd take the rose—even if it was down to its last petal. Beautiful, cold, white marble leaves me—well, just a little cold.

Roses are warm and fragrant, and almost every flower I know, wild or cultivated, has its own unique quality, whether it be subtle fragrance or arresting colour or loveliness of design. Unfortunately, winter has come to the Himalayas, and the hillsides are now brown and dry, the only colour being that of the red sorrel growing from the limestone rocks. Even my small garden looks rather forlorn, with the year's last dark-eyed nasturtium looking every bit like the Lone Ranger surveying the surrounding wilderness from his saddle. The marigolds have dried in the sun, and tomorrow I will gather the seed. The beanstalk that grew rampant during the monsoon is now down to a few yellow leaves and empty bean pods.

'This won't do,' I told myself the other day. 'I must have flowers!'

Prem, who had been down to the valley town of Dehra the previous week, had made me even more restless, because he had spoken of masses of sweet peas in full bloom in the garden of one of the town's public schools. Down in the plains, winter is the best time for gardens, and I remembered my grandmother's house in Dehra, with its long rows of hollyhocks, neatly staked sweet peas, and beds ablaze with red salvia and antirrhinum. Neither Grandmother nor the house are there anymore, but surely there are other beautiful gardens, I mused, and maybe I could visit the school where Prem had seen the sweet peas. It was a long time since I had enjoyed their delicate fragrance.

So I took the bus down the hill, and throughout the two-hour journey I dozed and dreamt of gardens—cottage gardens in the English countryside, tropical gardens in Florida, Mughal Gardens in Kashmir, the Hanging Gardens of Babylon! What had they really been like, I wondered.

And then we were in Dehra, and I got down from the bus and walked down the dusty, busy road to the school Prem had told me about.

It was encircled by a high wall, and, tiptoeing, I could see playing fields and extensive school buildings and, in the far distance, a dollop of colour that *may* have been a garden. Prem's eyesight was obviously better than mine!

I made my way to a wrought-iron gate that would have done justice to a medieval fortress, and found it chained and locked. On the other side stood a tough-looking guard, with a rifle.

'May I enter?' I asked.

'Sorry, sir. Today is holiday. No school today.'

'I don't want to attend classes. I want to see sweet peas.'

'Kitchen is on the other side of the ground.'

'Not green peas. Sweet peas. I'm looking for the garden.'

'I am guard here.'

'*Garden.*'

'No garden, only guard.'

I tried telling him that I was an old boy of the school and that I was visiting the town after a long interval. This was true up to a point, because I had once been admitted to this very school, and after one day's attendance had insisted on going back to my old school. The guard was unimpressed. And perhaps it was poetic justice that the gates were barred to me now.

Disconsolate, I strolled down the main road, past a garage, a cinema, and a row of eating houses and tea shops. Behind the shops there seemed to be a park of sorts, but you couldn't see much of it from the road because of the buildings, the press of people, and the passing trucks and buses. But I found the entrance, unbarred this time, and struggled through patches of overgrown shrubbery until, like Alice after finding the golden key to the little door in the wall, I looked upon a lovely little garden.

There were no sweet peas, and the small fountain was dry. But around it, filling a large circular bed, were masses of bright yellow California poppies.

They stood out like sunshine after rain, and my heart leapt as Wordsworth's must have, when he saw his daffodils. I found myself oblivious to the sounds of the bazaar and the road, just as the people outside seemed oblivious to this little garden. It was as though it had been waiting here all this time, waiting for me to come by and discover it.

I am fortunate. Something like this is always happening to me. As Grandmother often said, 'When one door closes, another door opens.' And while one gate had been closed upon the sweet peas, another had opened on California poppies.

GENTLE SHADE BY DAY

Those who have spent time in non-air-conditioned parts of India will remember with gratitude those gracious trees that provide shade and shelter during the summer months—the banyan, peepul, mango, neem and others. Coastal dwellers are not so fortunate for there is not much shade to be had from a palm tree unless you keep moving in its long but insubstantial shadow.

I am not surprised that the sages of old were given to sitting beneath the peepul tree. They might have had various religious reasons for calling it sacred but I am sure there was a good practical reason as well. Few trees provide a cooler shade than it does. Even on the stillest of days, the peepul leaves are forever twirling and with thousands of leaves spinning like tops, there is quite a breeze for anyone sitting below.

However, there are warnings about peepul trees—'Gentle shade by day and terror by night!' During the night the tree is said to be alive with various spirits, most of them inimical to man. One is advised not to sleep beneath it for this is construed by a ghost as an invitation to jump down your throat and take possession of you, or at the very least ruin your digestion.

It is also said to be unlucky to sleep beneath a tamarind, but I have often reclined in the pleasant shade of this noble tree and have come to no harm. A famous tamarind stands over the tomb of Tansen, the great musician and singer of Akbar's court at Gwalior. Its leaves, though bitter, are eaten by singers to improve their voices.

A mango grove is a wonderful place for an afternoon siesta. But if the mangoes are ripening, there is usually a great deal of activity going on with parrots, crows, monkeys and small boys, all attempting to evade the watchman who uses an empty kerosene tin as a drum to try and frighten them away. So it's not the ideal place for a nap then, but the shade under a mango grove is dark, deep and very soothing.

The banyan tree with its aerial roots represents the matted hair of Lord Shiva. There is always shade and space beneath a venerable old banyan. It is still a popular community centre in our Indian villages but is becoming a rarity in cities simply because it covers so large an area. And if you cut its aerial roots the tree topples over. Other handsome trees related to the banyan are the pilkhan and the chilkhan, large spreading evergreens, both quite noticeable on some of New Delhi's wider avenues.

The neem is a tall tree, but its numerous branches give it a shady head. One of my greatest pleasures is to walk beneath an avenue of neem trees after a shower of rain. As the fallen berries are crushed underfoot they give out a sharp heady fragrance, which I find exhilarating. Apart from its medicinal uses, the tree is connected in legends with the Sun God as in the story of *Neembarak*. 'The Sun in a Neem Tree' who invited to dinner a Bairagi tribal whose rules forbade him to eat anything except by daylight. When dinner was delayed after sundown, Suraj Narayan, the Sun God, obligingly descended from a neem tree and continued shining till dinner was over.

On this pleasant note I end this tribute, only adding that shade-giving trees symbolize the harmony between man and nature and that our ancestors in their devotion to trees and reverence for them, clearly showed that they knew what was good for them.

WHITE CLOUDS, GREEN MOUNTAINS

Towards the end of September, those few monsoon clouds that still linger over the Himalayas are no longer burdened with rain and are able to assume unusual shapes and patterns, chasing each other across the sky and disappearing in spectacular sunset formations.

I have always found this to be the best time of the year in the hills. The sun-drenched hillsides are still an emerald green; the air is crisp, but winter's bite is still a month or two away; and for those who still like to take to the open road on foot, there are springs, streams and waterfalls tumbling over rocks that remain dry for most of the year. The lizard that basked on a sun-baked slab of granite last May is missing, but in his place the spotted forktail trips daintily among the boulders in a stream; and the strident sound of the cicadas is gradually replaced by the gentler trilling of the crickets and grasshoppers.

Cicadas, as you probably know, make their music with their legs, which are moved like the bows of violins against their bodies. It's rather like an orchestra tuning up but never quite getting on with the overture or symphony. Aunt Ruby, who is a little deaf, can nevertheless hear the cicadas when they are at their loudest. She lives not far from a large boarding-school, and one day when I remarked that I could hear the school choir or choral group singing, she nodded and remarked: 'Yes, dear. They do it with their legs, don't they?'

Come to think of it, that school choir does sound a bit squeaky.

Now, more than at any other time of the year, the wildflowers come into their own.

The hillside is covered with a sward of flowers and ferns. Sprays of wild ginger, tangles of clematis, flat clusters of yarrow and lady's mantle. The datura grows everywhere with its graceful white balls and prickly fruits. And the wild woodbine provides the stems from which the village boys make their flutes.

Aroids are plentiful and attract attention by their resemblance to snakes with protruding tongues—hence the popular name, cobra lily. This serpent's tongue is a perfect landing-stage for flies etc., who, crawling over the male flowers in their eager search for the liquor that lies at the base of the spike (a liquor that is most appealing to their depraved appetites), succeed in fertilizing the female flowers as they proceed. We see that it is not only humans who become addicted to alcohol. Bears have been known to get drunk on the juice of rhododendron flowers, while bumble bees can be out-and-out dipsomaniacs.

One of the more spectacular cobra lilies, which rejoices in the name *Sauromotum Guttatum*—ask your nearest botanist what that means!—bears a solitary leaf and purple spathe. When the seeds form, it withdraws the spike underground; and when the rains are over and the soil is not too damp, it sends it up again covered with scarlet berries. In the opinion of the hill folk, the appearance of the red spike is more to be relied on as a forecast of the end of the monsoon than any meteorological expertise. Up here on the ranges that fall between the Jumna and the Bhagirathi (known as the Rawain), we can be perfectly sure of fine weather a fortnight after the fiery spike appears.

But it is the commelina, more than any other Himalayan flower, that takes my breath away. The secret is in its colour—a pure pristine blue that seems to reflect the deepest blue of the sky. Towards the end of the rains it appears as if from nowhere, graces the hillside for the space of about two weeks, and disappears again until the following monsoon.

When I see the first commelina, I stand dumb before it and the world stands still while I worship. So absorbed do I become in its delicate beauty that I begin to doubt the reality of everything else in the world.

But only for a moment. The blare of a truck's horn reminds me that I am still lingering on the main road leading out of the hill station. A cloud of dust and blasts of diesel fumes are further indications that reality takes many different forms, assailing all my senses at once! Even my commelina seems to shrink from the onslaught. But as it is still there, I take heart and leave the highway for a lesser road.

Soon I have left the clutter of the town behind. What did Aunt Ruby say the other day? 'Stand still for five minutes, and they will build a hotel on top of you.'

Wasn't it Lot's wife who was turned into a pillar of salt when she looked back at the doomed city that had been her home? I have an uneasy feeling that I will be turned into a pillar of cement if I look back, so I plod on along the road to Devsari, a kindly village in the valley. It will be some time before 'developers' and big money boys get here, for no one will go to live where there is no driveway!

A tea shop beckons. How would one manage in the hills without these wayside tea shops? Miniature inns, they provide food, shelter and even lodging to dozens at a time.

I tackle some buns that have a pre-Independence look about them. They are rock-hard, to match the environment, but I manage to swallow some of the jagged pieces with the hot sweet tea, which is good.

THE KIPLING ROAD

Remember the old road,
The steep stony path
That took us up from Rajpur,
Toiling and sweating
And grumbling at the climb,
But enjoying it all the same.
At first the hills were hot and bare,
But then there were trees near Jharipani
And we stopped at the Halfway House
And swallowed lungfuls of diamond-cut air.
Then onwards, upwards, to the town,
Our appetites to repair!

Well, no one uses the old road anymore.
Walking is out of fashion now.
And if you have a car to take you
Swiftly up the motor-road

Why bother to toil up a disused path?
You'd have to be an old romantic like me

To want to take that route again.
But I did it last year,
Pausing and plodding and gasping for air
Both road and I being a little worse for wear!
But I made it to the top and stopped to rest
And looked down to the valley and the silver stream
Winding its way towards the plains.
And the land stretched out before me, and the years fell
away,
And I was a boy again,
And the friends of my youth were there beside me,
And nothing had changed.

'Remember the Old Road'

As boys we would often trudge up from Rajpur to Mussoorie by the old bridle-path, the road that used to serve the hill station in the days before the motor road was built. Before 1900, the traveller to Mussoorie took a tonga from Saharanpur to Dehradun, spent the night at a Rajpur hotel, and the following day came up the steep seven-mile path on horseback, or on foot, or in a dandy (a crude palanquin) held aloft by two, sometimes four, sweating coolies.

The railway came to Dehradun in 1904, and a few years later the first motor car made it to Mussoorie, the motor road following the winding contours and hairpin bends of the old bullock-cart road. Rajpur went out of business; no one stopped there any more, the hotels became redundant, and the bridlepath was seldom used except by those of us who thought it would be fun to come up on foot.

For the first two or three miles you walked in the hot sun, along a treeless path. It was only at Jharipani (at approximately

4,000 ft.) that the oak forests began, providing shade and shelter. Situated on a spur of its own, was the Railways school, Oakgrove, still there today, providing a boarding-school education to the children of Railway personnel. My mother and her sisters came from a Railway family, and all of them studied at Oakgrove in the 1920s. So did a male cousin, who succumbed to cerebral malaria during the school term. In spite of the salubrious climate, mortality was high amongst school children. There were no cures then for typhoid, cholera, malaria, dysentery and other infectious diseases.

Above Oakgrove was Fairlawn, the palace of the Nepali royal family. There was a sentry box outside the main gate, but there was never any sentry in it, and on more than one occasion I took shelter there from the rain. Today it's a series of cottages, one of which belongs to *Outlook*'s editor, Vinod Mehra, who seeks shelter there from the heat and dust of Delhi.

From Jharapani we climbed to Barlowganj, where another venerable institution St George's College, crowns the hilltop. Then on to Bala Hissar, once the home-in-exile of an Afghan king, and now the grounds of Wynberg-Allen, another school. In later years I was to live near this school, and it was its then Principal, Rev W. Biggs, who told me that the bridle-path was once known as the Kipling Road.

Why was that, I asked. Had Kipling ever come up that way? Rev Biggs wasn't sure, but he referred me to Kim, and the chapter in which Kim and the Lama leave the plains for the hills. It begins thus:

> They had crossed the Siwaliks and the half-tropical Doon, left Mussoorie behind them, and headed north along the narrow hill-roads. Day after day they struck deeper into the huddled mountains, and day after day Kim watched the

lama return to a man's strength. Among the terraces of the Doon he had leaned on the boy's shoulder, ready to profit by wayside halts. Under the great ramp to Mussoorie he drew himself together as an old hunter faces a well remembered bank, and where he should have sunk exhausted swung his long draperies about him, drew a deep double-lungful of the diamond air, and walked as only a hillman can.

This description is accurate enough, but it is not evidence that Kipling actually came this way, and his geography becomes quite confusing in the subsequent pages—as Peter Hopkirk discovered when he visited Mussoorie a few years ago, retracing Kim's journeys for his book *Quest for Kim*. Hopkirk spent some time with me in this little room where I am now writing, but we were unable to establish the exact route that Kim and the Lama took after traversing Mussoorie. Presumably they had come up the bridle-path. But then? After that, Kipling becomes rather vague.

Mussoorie does not really figure in Rudyard Kipling's prose or poetry. The Simla Hills were his beat. As a journalist he was a regular visitor to Simla, then the summer seat of the British Raj.

But last year my Swiss friend, Anilees Goel, brought me proof that Kipling had indeed visited Mussoorie. Among his unpublished papers and other effects in the Library of Congress, there exists an album of photographs, which includes two of the Charleville Hotel, Mussoorie, where he had spent the summer of 1888. On a photograph of the office he had inscribed these words:

And there were men with a thousand wants
And women with babes galore
But the dear little angels in Heaven know
That Wutzler never swore.

Wutzler was the patient, long-suffering manager of this famous hotel, now the premises of the Lal Bahadur Shastri National Academy of Administration.

A second photograph is inscribed with the caption 'Quarters at the Charleville, April July 88', and carries this verse:

A burning sun in cloudless skies
    and April dies,
A dusty Mall—three sunsets splendid
    and May is ended,
Grey mud beneath-grey cloud o'erhead
    and June is dead.
A little bill in late July
    And then we fly.

Pleasant enough, but hardly great verse, and I'm not surprised that Kipling did not publish these lines.

However, we now know that he came to Mussoorie and spent some time here, and that he would have come up by the old bridle-path (there was no other way except by bullock-cart on the long and tortuous cast road), and Rev Biggs and others were right in calling it the Kipling Road, although officially that was never its name.

As you climb up from Barlowganj, you pass a number of pretty cottages—May Cottage, Wakefield, Ralston Manor, Wayside Hall—and these old houses all have stories to tell, for they have stood mute witness to the comings and goings of all manner of people.

Take Ralston Manor. It was witness to an impromptu cremation, probably Mussoorie's first European cremation, in the late 1890s. There is a small chapel in the grounds of Ralston, and the story goes that a Mr and Mrs Smallman had been living in the house, and Mr Smallman had expressed a wish to be cremated at his death. When he died, his widow decided to observe his wishes and had her servants build a funeral pyre in the garden. The cremation was well underway when someone rode by and looked in to see what was happening. The unauthorized cremation was reported to the authorities and Mrs Smallman had to answer some awkward questions. However, she was let off with a warning (a warning not to cremate any future husbands?) and later she built the little chapel on the site of the funeral pyre—in gratitude or as penance, or as a memorial, we are not told. But the chapel is still there, and this little tale is recorded in Chowkidar (Autumn 1995), the journal of the British Association for Cemeteries in South Asia (BACSA).

As we move further up the road, keeping to the right, we come to Wayside Hall and Wayside Cottage, which have the advantage of an open sunny hillside and views to the north and east. I lived in the cottage for a couple of years, back in 1966–67, as a tenant of the Powell sisters who lived in the Hall.

There were three sisters, all in their seventies; they had survived their husbands. Annie, the eldest, had a son who lived abroad; Martha, the second, did not have children; Dr Simmonds, the third sister, had various adopted children who came to see her from time to time. They were God-fearing, religious folk, but not bigots; never chided me for not going to church. Annie's teas were marvellous; snacks and savouries in abundance.

They kept a beautiful garden.

'Why go to church?' I said. 'Your garden is a church.'

In spring and summer it was awash with poppies, petunia, phlox, larkspur, calendula, snapdragons and other English flowers. During the monsoon, the gladioli took over, while magnificent dahlias reared up from the rich foliage. During the autumn came zinnias and marigolds and cosmos. And even during the winter months there would be geraniums and primulae blooming in the verandah.

Honeysuckle climbed the wall outside my window, filling my bedroom with its heady scent. And wisteria grew over the main gate. There was perfume in the air.

Annie herself smelt of freshly baked bread. Dr Simmonds smelt of Pears' baby soap. Martha smelt of apples. All good smells, emanating from good people.

Although they lived on their own, without any men on the premises, they never felt threatened or insecure. Mussoorie was a safe place to live in then, and still is to a great extent, much safer than towns in the plains, where the crime rate keeps pace with the population growth.

Annie's son, Gerald, then in his sixties, did come out to see them occasionally. He had been something of a shikari in his youth—or so he claimed—and told me he could call up a panther from the valley without any difficulty. To do this, he made a contraption out of an old packing-case, with a hole bored in the middle, then he passed a length of thick wire through the hole, and by moving the wire backwards and forward produced a sound not dissimilar to the sawing, coughing sound made by a panther during the mating season. (Incidentally, a panther and a leopard are the same animal.)

Gerry invited me to join him on a steep promontory overlooking a little stream. I did so with some trepidation. Hunting had never been my forte, and normally I preferred to go along with Ogden Nash's dictum, 'If you meet a panther, don't anther!'

However, Gerry's gun looked powerful enough, and I

believed him when he told me he was a crack shot. I have always taken people at their word. One of my failings I suppose.

Anyway, we positioned ourselves on this ledge, and Gerry started producing panther noises with his box. His Master's Voice would have been proud of it. Nothing happened for about twenty minutes, and I was beginning to lose patience when we were answered by the cough and grunt of what could only have been a panther. But we couldn't see it! Gerry produced a pair of binoculars and trained them on some distant object below, which turned out to be a goat. The growling continued, and then it was just above us! The panther had made a detour and was now standing on a rock and staring down, no doubt wondering which of us was making such attractive mating calls.

Gerry swung round, raised his gun and fired. He missed by a couple of feet, and the panther bounded away, no doubt disgusted with the proceedings.

We returned to Wayside Hall, and revived ourselves with brandy and soda.

'We'll get it next time, old chap,' said Gerry. But although we tried, the panther did not put in another appearance. Gerry's panther call sounded genuine enough, but neither he nor I nor his wired box looked anything like a female panther.

HAROLD: OUR HORNBILL

Harold's mother, like all good hornbills, was the most careful of wives. His father was the most easy-going of husbands. In January, long before the flame tree flowered, Harold's father took his wife into a great hole high in the tree trunk, where his father and his father's father had taken their brides at the same time every year.

In this weather-beaten hollow, generation upon generation of hornbills had been raised. Harold's mother, like those before her, was enclosed within the hole by a sturdy wall of earth, sticks, and dung.

Harold's father left a small hole in the centre of this wall to enable him to communicate with his wife whenever he felt like a chat. Walled up in her uncomfortable room, Harold's mother was a prisoner for over two months. During this period an egg was laid, and Harold was born.

In his naked boyhood Harold was no beauty. His most promising feature was his flaming red bill, matching the blossoms of the flame tree which was now ablaze, heralding the summer. He had a stomach that could never be filled, despite the best efforts of his parents who brought him pieces of jackfruit and berries from the banyan tree.

As he grew bigger, the room became more cramped, and one day his mother burst through the wall, spread out her wings and sailed over the tree-tops. Her husband was glad to see her about. He played with her, expressing his delight with deep gurgles and throaty chuckles. Then they repaired the wall of the nursery, so that Harold would not fall out.

Harold was quite happy in his cell, and felt no urge for freedom. He was putting on weight and a philosophy of his own. Then something happened to change the course of his life.

One afternoon he was awakened from his siesta by a loud thumping on the wall, a sound quite different from that made by his parents. Soon the wall gave way, and there was something large and yellow and furry staring at him—not his parents' bills, but the hungry eyes of a civet cat.

Before Harold could be seized, his parents flew at the cat, both roaring lustily and striking out with their great bills. In the ensuing melee, Harold tumbled out of his nest and landed on our garden path.

Before the cat or any predator could get to him, Grandfather picked him up and took him to the sanctuary of the verandah.

Harold had lost some wing feathers and did not look as though he would be able to survive on his own, so we made an enclosure for him on our front verandah. Grandfather and I took over the duties of his parents.

Harold had a simple outlook, and once he had got over some early attacks of nerves, he began to welcome the approach of people. Grandfather and I meant the arrival of food and he greeted us with craning neck, quivering open bill, and a loud, croaking, 'Ka-ka-kaee!'

Fruit, insect or animal food, and green leaves were all

welcome. We soon dispensed with the enclosure, but Harold made no effort to go away; he had difficulty flying. In fact, he asserted his tenancy rights, at least as far as the verandah was concerned.

One afternoon a verandah tea party was suddenly and alarmingly convulsed by a flash of black and white and noisy flapping. And behold, the last and only loaf of bread had been seized and carried off to his perch near the ceiling.

Harold was not beautiful by Hollywood standards. He had it a small body and a large head. But he was good-natured and friendly, and he remained on good terms with most members of the household during his lifetime of twelve years.

Harold's best friends were those who fed him, and he was willing even to share his food with us, sometimes trying to feed me with his great beak.

While I turned down his offers of beetles and similar delicacies, I did occasionally share a banana with him. Eating was a serious business for Harold, and if there was any delay at mealtimes he would summon me with raucous barks and vigorous bangs of his bill on the woodwork of the kitchen window.

Having no family, profession or religion, Harold gave much time and thought to his personal appearance. He carried a rouge pot on his person and used it very skilfully as an item of his morning toilet.

This rouge pot was a small gland situated above the roots of his tail feathers; it produced a rich yellow fluid. Harold would dip into his rouge pot from time to time and then rub the colour over his feathers and the back of his neck. It would come off on my hands whenever I touched him.

Harold would toy with anything bright or glittering, often

swallowing it afterwards.

He loved bananas and dates and balls of boiled rice. I would throw him the rice balls, and he would catch them in his beak, toss them in the air, and let them drop into his open mouth.

He perfected this trick of catching things, and in time I taught him to catch a tennis ball thrown with some force from a distance of fifteen yards. He would have made a great baseball catcher or an excellent slip fielder. On one occasion he seized a rupee coin from me (a week's pocket money in those days) and swallowed it neatly.

Only once did he really misbehave. That was when he removed a lighted cigar from the hand of an American cousin who was visiting us. Harold swallowed the cigar. It was a moving experience for Harold, and an unnerving one for our guest.

Although Harold never seemed to drink any water, he loved the rain. We always knew when it was going to rain because Harold would start chuckling to himself about an hour before the first raindrops fell.

This used to irritate Aunt Ruby. She was always being caught in the rain. Harold would be chuckling when she left the house. And when she returned, drenched to the skin, he would be in fits of laughter.

As storm clouds would gather, and gusts of wind would shake the banana trees, Harold would get very excited, and his chuckle would change to an eerie whistle.

'Wheee...wheee,' he would scream, and then, as the first drops of rain hit the verandah steps, and the scent of the fresh earth passed through the house, he would start roaring with pleasure.

The wind would carry the rain into the verandah, and Harold would spread out his wings and dance, tumbling about like a circus clown. My grandparents and I would come out on the verandah and share his happiness.

Many years later, I still miss Harold's raucous bark and the banging of his great bill. If there is a heaven for good hornbills, I sincerely hope he is getting all the summer showers he could wish for, and plenty of tennis balls to catch.

ROAD TO BADRINATH

If you have travelled up the Mandakini valley, and then cross over into the valley of the Alaknanda, you are immediately struck by the contrast. The Mandakini is gentler, richer in vegetation, almost pastoral in places; the Alaknanda is awesome, precipitous, threatening, and seemingly inhospitable to those who must live and earn a livelihood in its confines.

Even as we left Chamoli and began the steady, winding climb to Badrinath, the nature of the terrain underwent a dramatic change. No longer did green fields slope gently down to the riverbed. Here they clung precariously to rocky slopes and ledges that grew steeper and narrower, while the river below, impatient to reach its confluence with the Bhagirathi at Deoprayag, thundered along a narrow gorge.

Badrinath is one of the four Dhams, or four most holy places in India (the other three are Rameshwaram, Dwarka and Jagannath Puri). For the pilgrim travelling to his holiest of holies, the journey is exciting, possibly even uplifting; but for those who live permanently on these crags and ridges, life is harsh, a struggle from one day to the next. No wonder so many young men from Garhwal make their way into the Army.

Little grows on these rocky promontories; and what does is at the mercy of the weather. For most of the year the fields lie fallow. Rivers, unfortunately, run downhill and not uphill.

The harshness of this life, typical of much of Garhwal, was brought home to me at Pipalkoti, where we stopped for the night. Pilgrims stop here by the coachload, for the Garhwal Mandal Vikas Nigam's rest house is fairly capacious and small hotels and dharamsalas abound. Just off the busy road is a tiny hospital, and here, late in the evening, we came across a woman keeping vigil over the dead body of her husband. The body had been laid out on a bench in the courtyard. A few feet away the road was crowded with pilgrims in festival mood; no one glanced over the low wall to notice this tragic scene.

The woman came from a village near Helong. Earlier that day, finding her consumptive husband in a critical condition, she had decided to bring him to the nearest town for treatment. As he was frail and emaciated, she was able to carry him on her back for several miles until she reached the motor road. Then, at some expense, she engaged a passing taxi and brought him to Pipalkoti. But he was already dead when she reached the small hospital. There was no morgue; so she sat beside the body in the courtyard, waiting for dawn and the arrival of others from the village. A few men arrived next morning, and we saw them wending their way down to the cremation ground. We did not see the woman again. Her children were hungry and she had to hurry home to look after them.

Pipalkoti is hot (and pipal trees are conspicuous by their absence), but Joshimath, the winter resort of the Badrinath temple establishment, is about 6,000 ft above sea level and has an equable climate. It is now a fairly large town, and although the surrounding hills are rather bare, it does have one great tree that has survived the ravages of time. This is an ancient mulberry, known as the Kalpa-Vriksha (Immortal Wishing Tree), beneath which the great Sankaracharya meditated a few centuries ago. It is reputedly over two thousand years old, and is certainly larger than my modest four-roomed flat in Mussoorie. Sixty pilgrims holding hands might just about encircle its trunk.

I have seen some big trees, but this is certainly the oldest and broadest of them. I am glad that Sankaracharya meditated beneath it and thus ensured its preservation. Otherwise it might well have gone the way of other great trees and forests that once flourished in this area.

A small boy reminds me that it is a Wishing Tree, so I make my wish. I wish that other trees might prosper like this.

'Have you made a wish?' I ask the boy.

'I wish that you will give me one rupee,' he says.

His wish comes true with immediate effect. Mine lies in an uncertain future. But he has given me a lesson in wishing.

Joshimath has to be a fairly large place because most of Badrinath arrives here in November, when the shrine is snowbound for six months. Army and PWD structures also dot the landscape. This is no carefree hill resort, but it has all the amenities for making a short stay quite pleasant and interesting. Perched on the steep mountainside above the junction of the Alaknanda and Dhauli rivers, it is now vastly different from what it was when Frank Smythe visited it fifty years ago and described it as 'an ugly little place...straggling unbeautifully over the hillside'. Primitive little shops line the main street, which is roughly paved in places and in others has been deeply channelled by the monsoon rains. The pilgrims spend the night in single-storeyed rest houses, not unlike the hovels provided for the Kentish hop-pickers of former days, and are filthy and evil-smelling'.

Those were Joshimath's former days. It is a different place today, with small hotels, modern shops, a cinema; and its growth and comparative modernity dates from the early sixties when the old pilgrim footpath gave way to the motor road which takes the traveller all the way to Badrinath. No longer does the weary, footsore pilgrim sink gratefully down in the shade of the Kalpa-Vriksha. He alights from his bus or luxury coach and drinks a Cola or a Thums-up at one of the many small restaurants on the roadside.

Contrast this comfortable journey with the pilgrimage fifty years ago. Frank Smythe again: 'So they venture on their pilgrimage... Some borne magnificently by coolies, some toiling along in rags, some almost crawling, preyed on by disease and distorted by dreadful deformities... Europeans who have read and travelled cannot conceive what goes on in the minds of these simple folk, many of them from the agricultural parts of India. Wonderment and fear must be the prime ingredients. So the pilgrimage becomes an adventure. Unknown dangers threaten the broad well-made path, at any moment the Gods, who hold the rocks in leash, may unloose their wrath upon the hapless passerby. To the European it is a walk to Badrinath, to the Hindu pilgrim it is far, far more.'

Above Vishnuprayag, Smythe left the Alaknanda and entered the Bhyundar valley, a botanist's paradise, which he called the Valley of Flowers. He fell in love with the lush meadows of this high valley and made it known to the world. It continues to attract the botanist and trekker. Primulas of subtle shades, wild geraniums, saxifrages clinging to the rocks, yellow and red potentillas, snow-white anemones, delphiniums, violets, wild roses, all these and many more flourish there, capturing the mind and heart of the flower-lover.

'Impossible to take a step without crushing a flower.' This may not be true any more, for many footsteps have trodden the Bhyundar in recent years. There are other areas in Garhwal where the hills are rich in flora—the Har-ki-Doon, Harsil, Tungnath, and the Khiraun valley where the Balsam grows to a height of eight feet—but the Bhyundar has both a variety and a concentration of wild flowers, especially towards the end of the monsoon. It would be no exaggeration to call it one of the most beautiful valleys in the world.

The Bhyundar is a digression for lovers of mountain scenery; but the pilgrim keeps his eyes fixed on the ultimate goal—Badrinath, where the gods dwell and where salvation is to be found.

There are still a few who do it the hard way—mostly those who have taken sanyas and renounced the world. Here is one hardy soul doing penance. He stretches himself out on the ground, draws himself up to a standing position, then flattens himself out again. In this manner he will proceed from Badrinath to Rishikesh, oblivious of the sun and rain, the dust from passing buses, the sharp gravel of the footpath.

Others are not so hardy. One saffron-robed scholar speaking fair English asks us for a lift to Badrinath, and we find a space for him. He rewards us with a long and involved commentary on the Vedas, which lasts through the remainder of the journey. His special field of study, he informs us, is the part played by aeronautics in Vedic literature.

'And what,' I ask him, 'is the connection between the two?'

He looks at me pityingly.

'It is what I am trying to find out,' he replies.

The road drops to Pandukeshwar and rises again, and all the time I am scanning the horizon for the forests of the Badrinath region I had read about many years ago in Eraser's *Himalaya Mountains*. Walnuts growing up to 9,000 ft, deodars and Bilka up to 9,500 ft, and Amesh and Kiusu fir to a similar height—but, apart from strands of long leaved and excelsia pine, I do not see much, certainly no deodars. What has happened to them, I wonder. An endless variety of trees delighted us all the way from Dugalbeta to Mandal, a well-protected area, but here on the high ridges above the Alaknanda, little seems to grow: or, if ever anything did, it has long since been bespoiled or swept away.

Finally we reach the windswept, barren valley which harbours Badrinath—a growing township, thriving, lively, but somewhat dwarfed by the snow-capped peaks that tower above it. As at Joshimath, there is no dearth of hostelries and dharamsalas. Even so, every hotel or rest house is overcrowded. It is the height of the pilgrim season, and pilgrims, tourists and mendicants of every description throng the river-front.

Just as Kedar is the most sacred of the Shiva temples in the Himalayas, similarly Badrinath is the supreme place of worship for the Vaishnav sects.

According to legend, when Sankaracharya in his Digvijaya travels visited the Mana valley, he arrived at the Narada-Kund and found fifty different images lying in its waters. These he rescued, and when he had done so, a voice from Heaven said: 'These are the images for the Kaliyug, establish them here.' Sankaracharya accordingly placed them beneath a mighty tree which grew there and whose shade extended from Badrinath to Nandprayag, a distance of over eighty miles. Close to it was the hermitage of Nar-Nandprayag (or Arjuna and Krishna), and in course of time temples were built in honour of these and other manifestations of Vishnu. It was here that Vishnu appeared to his followers in person, as four-armed, crested and adorned with pearls and garlands. The faithful, it is said, can still see him on the peak of Nilkantha, on the great Kumbha day. It is in fact the Nilkantha peak that dominates this crater-like valley, where a few hardy thistles and nettles manage to survive. Like cacti in the desert, the pricklier forms of life seem best equipped to live in a hostile environment.

Nilkantha means blue-necked, an allusion to Lord Shiva's swallowing of a poison meant to destroy the world. The poison remained in his throat, which was rendered blue thereafter. It is a majestic and awe-inspiring peak, soaring to a height of 21,640 ft. As its summit is only five miles from Badrinath, it is justly held in reverence. From its ice-clad pinnacle, three great ridges sweep down, of which the south terminates in the Alaknanda valley.

On the evening of our arrival we could not see the peak, as it was hidden in cloud. Badrinath itself was shrouded in mist. But we made our way to the temple, a gaily decorated building, about fifty feet high, with a gilded roof. The image of Vishnu, carved in black stone, stands in the centre of the sanctum, opposite the door, in a Dhyana posture. An endless stream of people pass through the temple to pay homage and emerge the better for their proximity to the divine.

From the temple, flights of steps lead down to the rushing river and to the hot springs which emerge just above it. Another road leads through a long but tidy bazaar where pilgrims may buy mementos of their visit—from sacred amulets to pictures of the gods in vibrant technicolour. Here at last I am free to indulge my passion for cheap rings, with none to laugh at my foible. There are all kinds, from rings designed like a coiled serpent (my favourite) to twisted bands of copper and iron and others containing the pictures of gods, gurus and godmen.

They do not cost more than two or three rupees each, and so I am able to fill my pockets. I never wear these rings. I simply hoard them away. My friends are convinced that in a previous existence I was a jackdaw, seizing upon and hiding away any kind of bright and shiny object!

India is a land of crowds, and it is no different at Badrinath where people throng together, all in good spirits. Hindus enjoy their religion. Whether bathing in cold streams or hot springs, or tramping from one sacred mountain shrine to another, they are united in their wish to experience something of the magic and mystique of the gods and glories of another epoch.

Even those who have renounced the world appear to be cheerful—like the young woman from Gujarat who had taken sanyas, and who met me on the steps below the temple. She gave me a dazzling smile and passed me an exercise book. She had taken a vow of silence; but being, I think, of an extrovert nature, she seemed eager to remain in close communication with the rest of humanity, and did so by means of written questions and answers. Hence the exercise book. Together we filled three pages of it before she told me that she wished to proceed on pilgrimage to Amarnath but was short of funds. With help from my generous companion, we made her a donation, and with a flashing smile of thanks she left us and was lost in the crowd.

Although at Badrinath I missed the sound of birds and the presence of trees, there were other compensations. It was good to be part of the happy throng at its colourful little temple and to see the sacred river close to its source. And early next morning I was rewarded with the loveliest experience of all.

Opening the window of my room and glancing out, I saw the rising sun touch the snow-clad summit of Nilkantha. At first the snows were pink; then they turned to orange and gold. All sleep vanished as I gazed up in wonder at that magnificent pinnacle in the sky. And had Lord Vishnu appeared just then on the summit, I would not have been in the least surprised.

IN SEARCH OF SWEET PEAS

If someone were to ask me to choose between writing an essay on the Taj Mahal or on the last rose of the summer, I'd take the rose—even if it was down to its last petal. Beautiful, cold, white marble leaves me—well, just a little cold… Roses are warm and fragrant, and almost every flower I know, wild or cultivated, has its own unique quality, whether it be subtle fragrance or arresting colour or liveliness of design. Unfortunately, winter has come to the Himalayas, and the hillsides are now brown and dry, the only colour being that of the red sorrel growing from the limestone rocks. Even my small garden looks rather forlorn, with the year's last dark-eyed nasturtium looking every bit like the Lone Ranger surveying the surrounding wilderness from his saddle. The marigolds have dried in the sun and tomorrow I will gather the seeds. The beanstalk that grew rampant during the monsoon is now down to a few yellow leaves and empty bean-pods.

'This won't do,' I told myself the other day. 'I must have flowers.' Prem, who had been to the valley town of Dehra the previous week, had made me even more restless, because he had spoken of masses of sweet peas in full bloom in the garden of one of the town's public schools. Down in the plains, winter is the best time for gardens, and I remembered my grandmother's house in Dehra, with its long rows of hollyhocks, neatly-stalked sweet peas and beds ablaze with red salvia and antirrhinum. Neither grandmother nor the house are there anymore. But surely there are other beautiful gardens, I mused, and maybe I could visit the school where Prem had seen the sweet peas. It was a long time since I had enjoyed their delicate fragrance.

So I took the bus down the hill, and throughout the two-hour journey, I dozed and dreamt of gardens—cottage gardens in the English countryside, tropical gardens in Florida, Mughal gardens in Kashmir, the Hanging Gardens of Babylon—what had they been like, I wondered.

And then we were in Dehra, and I got down from the bus and walked down the dusty, busy road to the school Prem had told me about.

It was encircled by a high wall, and, tip-toeing, I could see playing fields and extensive school buildings and, in the far distance, a dollop of colour which may have been a garden. Prem's eyesight was obviously better than mine.

Anyway, I made my way to a wrought iron gate that would have done justice to a medieval fortress, and found it chained and locked. On the other side stood a tough looking guard, with a rifle.

'May I enter?' I asked.

'Sorry, sir, today is holiday. No school today.'

'I don't want to attend classes, I want to see the sweet peas.'

'Kitchen is on the other side of the ground.'

'Not green peas. Sweet peas. I'm looking for the garden.'

'I am guard here.'

'Garden.'

'No garden, only guard.'

I tried telling him that I was an old boy of the school and that I was visiting the town after a long interval. This was true up to a point, because I had once been admitted to this very school, and after one day's attendance had insisted on going back to my old school. The guard was unimpressed. And perhaps it was poetic justice that the gates were barred to me now.

Disconsolate, I strolled down the main road, past a garage, a cinema, a row of cheap eating houses and tea shops. Behind the shops there seemed to be a park of sorts, but you couldn't see much of it from the road because of the buildings, the press of the people, and the passing trucks and buses. But I found the entrance, unbarred this time, and struggled through patches of overgrown shrubbery until, like Alice after finding the golden key to the little door in the wall, I looked upon a lovely little garden.

There were no sweet peas, true, and the small fountain was dry. But around it, filling a large circular bed, were masses of bright yellow Californian poppies!

They stood out like sunshine after the rain, and my heart leapt as Wordsworth's must have done when he saw his daffodils. I found myself oblivious to the sounds of the bazaar and the road, just as the people outside seemed oblivious to this little garden. It was as though it had been waiting here all the time. Waiting for me to come by and discover it.

I am very fortunate. Something like this is always happening to me. As grandmother often said, 'When one door closes, another door opens.' And while one gate had been closed upon the sweet peas, another had opened on Californian poppies.

◆

Trees make you feel younger. And the older the tree, the younger you feel.

Whenever I pass beneath the old tamarind tree standing sentinel in the middle of Dehra's busiest street crossing, the years fall away and I am a boy again, sitting on the railing that circled the tree, while across the road, Granny ascended the steps of the Allahabad Bank, where she kept her savings.

The bank is still there, but the surroundings have changed, the traffic and the noise is far greater than it used to be, and I wouldn't dream of sauntering across the road as casually as I would have done in those days. The press of people is greater too, reflecting the tenfold increase in population that has taken place in this and other north Indian towns during the last forty years. But the old tamarind has managed to survive it all. As long as it stands, as long as its roots still cling to Dehra's rich soil, I shall feel confident that my own roots are well-embedded in this old valley town.

There was a time when almost every Indian village had its spreading banyan tree, in whose generous shade, schoolteachers conducted open-air classes, village elders met to discuss matters of moment, and itinerant merchants spread out their ware. Squirrels, birds of many kinds, flying-foxes, and giant beetles, are just some, of the many inhabitants of this gentle giant. Ancient banyan trees are still to be found in some parts of the country; but as villages grow into towns, and towns into cities, the banyan is gradually disappearing. It needs a lot of space for its aerial roots to travel and support it, and space is now at a premium.

If you can't find a banyan, a mango grove is a wonderful place for a quiet stroll or an afternoon siesta. In traditional paintings, it is often the haunt of young lovers. But if the mangoes are ripening, there is not much privacy in a mango grove. Parrots, crows, monkeys and small boys are all attempting to evade the watchman who uses an empty gasoline tin as a drum to frighten away these intruders.

The mango and the banyan don't grow above the foothills, and here in the mountains, the more familiar trees are the Himalayan oaks, horse-chestnuts, rhododendrons, pines and deodars. The deodar (from the Sanskrit dev-dar, meaning Tree of God) resembles the cedar of Lebanon, and can grow to a great height in a few hundred years. There are a number of giant deodars on the outskirts of Mussoorie, where I live, and they make the town seem quite young. Mussoorie is only 160 years old. The deodars are at least twice that age.

These are gregarious trees—they like being among their own kind—and a forest of deodars is an imposing sight. When a mountain is covered with them, they look like an army on the march: The only kind of army one would like to see marching over the mountains! Although the world has already lost over half its forest cover, these sturdy giants look as though they are going to be around a long time, given half a chance.

The world's oldest trees, a species of pine, grow in California and have been known to live up to five thousand years. Is that why Californians look so young?

The oldest tree I have seen is an ancient mulberry growing at Joshimath, a small temple town in the Himalayas. It is known as the Kalp-Vriksha or Immortal Tree. The Hindu sage, Sankaracharya, is said to have meditated beneath it in the sixteenth century. These ancient sages always found a suitable tree beneath which they could meditate. The Buddha favoured a banyan tree, while Hindu ascetics are still to be found sitting cross-legged beneath peepal trees. Peepals are just right in summer, because the slender heart-shaped leaves catch the slightest breeze and send cool currents down to the thinker below.

Personally, I prefer contemplation to meditation. I am happy to stand back from the great mulberry and study its awesome proportions. Not a tall tree, but it has an immense girth—my three-room apartment in Mussoorie would have fitted quite snugly into it. A small temple beside the tree looked very tiny indeed, and the children playing among its protruding roots could have been kittens.

As I said, I'm not one for meditating beneath trees, but that's really because something always happens to me when I try. I don't know how the great sages managed, but I find it difficult to concentrate when a Rhesus monkey comes up to me and stares me in the face. Or when a horse-chestnut bounces off my head. Or when a cloud of pollen slides off the branch of a deodar and down the back of my shirt. Or when a woodpecker starts hammering away a few feet up the trunk from where I sit. I expect the great ones were immune to all this arboreal activity. I'm just a nature-lover, easily distracted by the caterpillar crawling up my leg.

And so I am happy to stand back and admire the 'good, green-hatted people', as a visitor from another planet described the trees in a story by R.L. Stevenson. Especially the old trees. They have seen a lot of odd humans coming and going, and they know I'm just a seventy-year-old boy without any pretensions to being a sage.

SACRED SHRINES ALONG THE WAY

Nandprayag: Where Rivers Meet

It's a funny thing, but long before I arrive at a place I can usually tell whether I am going to like it or not.

Thus, while I was still some twenty miles from the town of Pauri, I felt it was not going to be my sort of place; and sure enough, it wasn't. On the other hand, while Nandprayag was still out of sight, I knew I was going to like it. And I did.

Perhaps it's something on the wind—emanations of an atmosphere—that are carried to me well before I arrive at my destination. I can't really explain it, and no doubt it is silly to make judgements in advance. But it happens and I mention the fact for what it's worth.

As for Nandprayag, perhaps I'd been there in some previous existence, I felt I was nearing home as soon as we drove into this cheerful roadside hamlet, some little way above the Nandakini's confluence with the Alakananda river. A prayag is a meeting place of two rivers, and as there are many rivers in the Garhwal Himalayas, all linking up to join either the Ganga or the Jamuna, it follows that there are numerous prayags, in themselves places of pilgrimage as well as wayside halts enroute to the higher Hindu shrines at Kedarnath and Badrinath. Nowhere else in the Himalayas are there so many temples, sacred streams, holy places and holy men. Some little way above Nandprayag's busy little bazaar is the tourist rest-house, perhaps the nicest of the tourist lodges in this region. It has a well-kept garden surrounded by fruit trees and is a little distance from the general hubbub of the main road.

Above it is the old pilgrim path, on which you walked. Just a few decades ago, if you were a pilgrim intent on finding salvation at the abode of the gods, you travelled on foot all the way from the plains, covering about 200 miles in a couple of months. In those days people had the time, the faith and the endurance. Illness and misadventure often dogged their footsteps, but what was a little suffering if at the end of the day they arrived at the very portals of heaven? Some did not survive to make the return journey. Today's pilgrims may not be lacking in devotion, but most of them do expect to come home again.

Along the pilgrim path are several handsome old houses, set among mango trees and the fronds of the papaya and banana. Higher up the hill the pine forests commence, but down here it is almost subtropical. Nandprayag is only about 3,000 feet above sea level—a height at which the vegetation is usually quite lush provided there is protection from the wind.

In one of these double-storeyed houses lives Mr Devki Nandan, scholar and recluse. He welcomes me into his house and plies me with food till I am close to bursting. He has a great love for his little corner of Garhwal and proudly shows me his collection of clippings concerning this area. One of them is from a travelogue by Sister Nivedita—an Englishwoman, Margaret Noble, who became an interpreter of Hinduism to the West. Visiting Nandprayag in 1928, she wrote:

> Nandprayag is a place that ought to be famous for its
> beauty and order. For a mile or two before reaching it we
> had noticed the superior character of the agriculture and
> even some careful gardening of fruits and vegetables. The
> peasantry also, suddenly grew handsome, not unlike the
> Kashmiris. The town itself is new, rebuilt since the Gohna
> flood, and its temple stands far out across the fields on the
> shore of the Prayag. But in this short time a wonderful
> energy has been at work on architectural carvings, and
> the little place is full of gemlike beauties. Its temple is
> dedicated to Naga Takshaka. As the road crosses the river,
> I noticed two or three old Pathan tombs, the only traces
> of Mohammedanism that we had seen north of Srinagar
> in Garhwal.

Little has changed since Sister Nivedita's visit, and there is
still a small and thriving Pathan population in Nandprayag. In
fact, when I called on Mr Devki Nandan, he was in the act
of sending out Eid greetings to his Muslim friends. Some of
the old graves have disappeared in the debris from new road
cuttings; an endless business, this road-building. And as for the
beautiful temple described by Sister Nivedita, I was sad to learn
that it had been swept away by a mighty flood in 1970, when a
cloudburst and subsequent landslide on the Alakananda resulted
in great destruction downstream.

Mr Nandan remembers the time when he walked to the
small hill station of Pauri to join the old Messmore Mission
School, where so many famous sons of Garhwal received their
early education. It would take him four days to get to Pauri.
Now it is just four hours by bus. It was only after the Chinese

invasion of 1962 that there was a rush of road-building in the hill districts of northern India. Before that, everyone walked and thought nothing of it!

Sitting alone that same evening in the little garden of the rest house, I heard innumerable birds break into song. I did not see any of them, because the light was fading and the trees were dark, but there was the rather melancholy call of the hill dove, the insistent ascending trill of the koel, and much shrieking, whistling and twittering that I was unable to assign to any particular species.

Now, once again, while I sit on the lawn surrounded by zinnias in full bloom, I am teased by that feeling of having been here before, on this lush hillside, among the pomegranates and oleanders. Is it some childhood memory asserting itself? But as a child I never travelled in these parts.

True, Nandprayag has some affinity with parts of the Doon valley before it was submerged by a tidal wave of humanity. But in the Doon there is no great river running past your garden. Here there are two, and they are also part of this feeling of belonging. Perhaps in some former life I did come this way, or maybe I dreamed about living here. Who knows? Anyway, mysteries are more interesting than certainties. Presently the room-boy joins me for a chat on the lawn. He is in fact running the rest house in the absence of the manager. A coach-load of pilgrims is due at any moment but until they arrive the place is empty and only the birds can be heard. His name is Janakpal and he tells me something about his village on the next mountain, where a leopard has been carrying off goats and cattle. He doesn't think much of the conservationists' law protecting leopards: Nothing can be done unless the animal becomes a man-eater!

A shower of rain descends on us, and so do the pilgrims, Janakpal leaves me to attend to his duties. But I am not left alone for long. A youngster with a cup of tea appears. He wants me to take him to Mussoorie or Delhi. He is fed up, he says, with washing dishes here.

'You are better off here,' I tell him sincerely. 'In Mussoorie you will have twice as many dishes to wash. In Delhi, ten times as many.'

'Yes, but there are cinemas there,' he says, 'and television, and videos.' I am left without an argument. Birdsong may have charms for me but not for the restless dish-washer in Nandprayag.

The rain stops and I go for a walk. The pilgrims keep to themselves but the locals are always ready to talk. I remember a saying (and it may have originated in these hills), which goes:

'All men are my friends. I have only to meet them.' In these hills, where life still moves at a leisurely and civilized pace, one is constantly meeting them.

The Magic of Tungnath

The mountains and valleys of Uttaranchal never fail to spring surprises on the traveller in search of the picturesque. It is impossible to know every corner of the Himalaya, which means that there are always new corners to discover; forest or meadow, mountain stream or wayside shrine.

The temple of Tungnath, at a little over 12,000 feet, is the highest shrine on the inner Himalayan range. It lies just below the Chandrashila peak. Some way off the main pilgrim routes, it is less frequented than Kedarnath or Badrinath, although it forms a part of the Kedar temple establishment. The priest here is a local man, a Brahmin from the village of Maku; the other Kedar temples have South Indian priests, a tradition begun by Sankaracharya, the eighth century Hindu reformer and revivalist.

Tungnath's lonely eminence gives it a magic of its own. To get there (or beyond), one passes through some of the most delightful temperate forest in the Garhwal Himalaya. Pilgrim, or trekker, or just plain rambler such as myself, one comes away a better person, forest-refreshed, and more aware of what the world was really like before mankind began to strip it bare.

Duiri Tal, a small lake, lies cradled on the hill above Okhimath, at a height of 8,000 feet. It was a favourite spot of one of Garhwal's earliest British Commissioners, J.H. Batten, whose administration continued for twenty years (1836–56).

He wrote:

> The day I reached there, it was snowing and young trees were laid prostrate under the weight of snow; the lake was frozen over to a depth of about two inches. There was no human habitation, and the place looked a veritable wilderness. The next morning when the sun appeared, the Chaukhamba and many other peaks extending as far as Kedarnath seemed covered with a new quilt of snow, as if close at hand. The whole scene was so exquisite that one could not tire of gazing at it for hours. I think a person who has a subdued settled despair in his mind would all of a sudden feel a kind of bounding and exalting cheerfulness which will be imparted to his frame by the atmosphere of Duiri Tal.

This feeling of uplift can be experienced almost anywhere along the Tungnath range. Duiri Tal is still some way off the beaten track, and anyone wishing to spend the night there should carry a tent; but further along this range, the road ascends to Dugalbeta (at about 9,000 feet) where a PWD rest house, gaily painted, has come up like some exotic orchid in the midst of a lush meadow topped by excelsia pines and pencil cedars. Many an official who has stayed here has rhapsodized on the charms of Dugalbeta; and if you are unofficial (and therefore not entitled to *stay* in the bungalow), you can move on to Chopta, lusher still, where there is accommodation of a sort for pilgrims and other hardy souls. Two or three little tea-shops provide mattresses and quilts. The Garhwal Mandal is putting up a rest house. These tourist rest houses of Garhwal are a great boon to the traveller; but during the pilgrim season (May/June) they are filled to overflowing, and if you turn up unexpectedly you might have to take your pick of tea-shop or 'dharamshala': something of a lucky dip, since they vary a good deal in comfort and cleanliness.

The trek from Chopta to Tungnath is only three and a half miles, but in that distance one ascends about 3,000 feet, and the pilgrim may be forgiven for feeling that at places he is on a perpendicular path. Like a ladder to heaven, I couldn't help thinking.

In spite of its steepness, my companion, the redoubtable Ganesh Saili, insisted that we take a shortcut. After clawing our way up tufts of alpine grass, which formed the rungs of our ladder, we were stuck and had to inch our way down again; so that the ascent of Tungnath began to resemble a game of Snakes and Ladders.

A tiny guardian-temple dedicated to Lord Ganesh spurred us on. Nor was I really fatigued; for the cold fresh air and the verdant greenery surrounding us was like an intoxicant. Myriads of wildflowers grow on the open slopes-buttercups, anemones, wild strawberries, forget-me-nots, rock-cress-enough to rival Bhyundar's 'Valley of Flowers' at this time of the year.

But before reaching these alpine meadows, we climb through rhododendron forest, and here one finds at least three species of this flower: the red-flowering tree rhododendron (found throughout the Himalaya between 6,000 feet and 10,000 feet); a second variety, the almatta, with flowers that are light red or rosy in colour; and the third chimul or white variety, found at heights ranging from between 10,000 and 13,000 feet. The chimul is a brushwood, seldom more than twelve feet high and growing slantingly due to the heavy burden of snow it has to carry for almost six months in the year.

These brushwood rhododendrons are the last trees we see on our ascent, for as we approach Tungnath the tree line ends and there is nothing between earth and sky except grass and rock and tiny flowers. Above us, a couple of crows dive-bomb a hawk, who does his best to escape their attentions. Crows are the world's great survivors. They are capable of living at any height and in any climate; as much at home in the back streets of Delhi as on the heights of Tungnath.

Another survivor up here at any rate, is the pika, a sort of mouse-hare, who looks like neither mouse nor hare but rather a tiny guinea-pig-small ears, no tail, grey-brown fur, and chubby feet. They emerge from their holes under the rocks to forage for grasses on which to feed. Their simple diet and thick fur enable them to live in extreme cold, and they have been found at 16,000 feet, which is higher than any other mammal lives. The Garhwalis call this little creature the runda—at any rate, that's what the temple priest called it, adding that it was not averse to entering houses and helping itself to grain and other delicacies. So perhaps there's more in it of mouse than of hare.

These little rundas were with us all the way from Chopta

to Tungnath; peering out from their rocks or scampering about on the hillside, seemingly unconcerned by our presence. At Tungnath' they live beneath the temple flagstones. The priest's grandchildren were having a game discovering their burrows; the rundas would go in at one hole and pop out at another they must have had a system of underground passages.

When we arrived, clouds had gathered over Tungnath, as they do almost every afternoon. The temple looked austere in the gathering gloom.

To some, the name 'rung' indicates 'lofty', from the position of the temple on the highest peak outside the main chain of the Himalaya; others derive it from the word 'tunga', that is 'to be suspended'—an allusion to the form under which the deity is worshipped here. The form is the Swayambhu Ling.

On Shivratri or Night of Shiva, the true believer may, 'with the eye of faith', see the lingam increase in size; but 'to the evil-minded no such favour is granted'. The temple, though not very large, is certainly impressive, mainly because of its setting and the solid slabs of grey granite from which it is built. The whole place somehow puts me in mind of Emily Bronte's *Wuthering Heights*—bleak, windswept, open to the skies. And as you look down from the temple at the little half-deserted hamlet that serves it in summer, the eye is met by grey slate roofs and piles of stones, with just a few hardy souls in residence—for the majority of pilgrims now prefer to spend the night down at Chopta.

Even the temple priest, attended by his son and grandsons, complains bitterly of the cold. To spend every day barefoot on those cold flagstones must indeed be hardship. I wince after five minutes of it, made worse by stepping into a puddle of icy water. I shall never make a good pilgrim; no rewards for me, in this world or the next. But the pandit's feet are literally thick-skinned; and the children seem oblivious to the cold. Still in October they must be happy to descend to Maku, their home village on the slopes below Dugalbeta.

It begins to rain as we leave the temple. We pass herds of sheep huddled in a ruined dharamshala. The crows are still rushing about the grey weeping skies, although the hawk has very sensibly gone away. A runda sticks his nose out from his hole, probably to take a look at the weather. There is a clap of thunder and he disappears, like the white rabbit in *Alice in Wonderland*. We are halfway down the Tungnath 'ladder' when it begins to rain quite heavily. And now we pass our first genuine pilgrims, a group of intrepid Bengalis who are heading straight into the storm. They are without umbrellas or raincoats, but they are not to be deterred. Oaks and rhododendrons flash past as we dash down the steep, winding path. Another short cut, and Ganesh Saili takes a tumble, but is cushioned by moss and buttercups. My wrist-watch strikes a rock and the glass is shattered. No matter. Time here is of little or no consequence. Away with time! Is this, I wonder, the 'bounding and exalting cheerfulness' experienced by Batten and now manifesting itself in me?

The tea-shop beckons. How would one manage in the hills without these wayside tea-shops? Miniature inns, they provide food, shelter and even lodging to dozens at a time. We sit on a bench between a Gujjar herdsman and a pilgrim who is too feverish to make the climb to the temple. He accepts my offer of an aspirin to go with his tea. We tackle some buns—rock-hard, to match our environment—and wash the pellets down with hot sweet tea.

There is a small shrine here, too, right in front of the tea-shop. It is a slab of rock roughly shaped like a lingam, and it is daubed with vermilion and strewn with offerings of wildflowers. The mica in the rock gives it a beautiful sheen.

I suppose Hinduism comes closest to being a nature religion.

Rivers, rocks, trees, plants, animals and birds, all play their part, both in mythology and in everyday worship. This harmony is most evident in these remote places, where gods and mountains coexist. Tungnath, as yet unspoilt by a materialistic society, exerts its magic on all who come here with an open mind and heart.

A VILLAGE IN GARHWAL

I wake up to what sounds like the din of a factory buzzer, but is in fact the music of a single vociferous cicada in the lime tree near my window.

Through the open window, I focus on a pattern of small, glossy lime leaves; then through them I see the mountains, the furthest Himalayas, striding away into an immensity of sky.

'In a thousand ages of the gods I could not tell thee of the glories of Himachal.' So confessed a Sanskrit poet at the dawn of Indian history. The sea has had Stevenson and Conrad, Melville and Hemingway, but the mountains have continued to defy the written word. We have climbed their highest peaks and crossed their most difficult passes, but still they keep their secrecy and reserve, remaining remote, mysterious and spirit-haunted.

No wonder, then, that the people who live on the mountain slopes in the mistfilled valleys of the Garhwal Himalayas have long since learned humility and patience. Deep in the crouching mist lie their villages, while climbing the mountain slopes are forests of rhododendron, pine and deodar, soughing in the wind from the ice-bound passes. Pale women plough, while their men go down to the plains in search of work, for little grows on the beautiful mountains.

When I think of Manjari village in Garhwal, I see a small river, a tributary of the Ganga, rushing along the bottom of a steep, rocky valley. On the banks of the river and on the terraced hill above are small fields of corn, barley, mustard, potatoes and onions. A few fruit trees, mostly apricot and peach, grow near the village. Some hillsides are rugged and bare, masses of quartz or granite. On hills exposed to the wind, only grass and small shrubs are able to obtain a foothold.

This landscape is typical of Garhwal, one of India's most northerly regions, with its massive snow ranges bordering on Tibet. Although thinly populated, Garhwal does not provide much of a living for its people.

'You have such beautiful scenery,' I said, after crossing the first range of hills.

'True,' said my friend, 'but we cannot eat the scenery.'

And yet these are cheerful sturdy people, with great powers of endurance. Somehow they manage to wrest a precarious living from the unhelpful, calcinated soil.

I am their guest for a few days. My friend Gajadhar has brought me home to his village above the Nayar river. My own home is in the hill station of Mussoorie, two day's journey to the west. We took a train across the Ganga and into the foothills, and then a bus—no, several buses—and finally, made dizzy by fast driving around hairpin bends, alighted at the small hill town of Lansdowne, chief recruiting centre for the Garhwal Rifles. Garhwal soldiers distinguished themselves fighting alongside British troops in both the World Wars, and they still form a high percentage of recruits to the Indian Army. The money orders they send home are the mainstay of the village economy.

Lansdowne is just over 6,000 ft in altitude. From there we

walked some twenty-five miles between sunrise and sunset, until we came to Manjari village clinging to the terraced slopes of the Dudhatoli range.

And this is my fourth morning in the village. Other mornings I woke to the throaty chuckles of the red-billed blue magpies, as they glided between oak tree and medlar, but today the cicada has drowned all birdsong. It is a little out of season for the cicadas, but perhaps the sudden warm spell in late September has deceived them into thinking it is again the mating season.

As usual, I am the last to get up. Gajadhar is exercising in the courtyard, going through an odd combination of yoga and Swedish exercises. With his sturdy physique and quick intelligence, I am sure he will realize his ambition of joining the Indian Army as an officer-cadet. He is proud of his family's army tradition, as indeed are most Garhwalis who remember that the first Indian to win the Victoria Cross (in World War I) was a Garhwali Rifleman Gabbar Singh Negi, who lost his life in the muddy fields of Flanders.

Gajadhar's younger brother Chakradhar, who is slim and fair with high cheekbones, is milking the family's buffalo. Normally he would be on his long walk to school, which is five miles away, but this being a holiday, he is able to stay home and help with the household chores.

His mother is lighting a fire. She is a handsome woman, even though her ears, weighed down by heavy silver earrings, have lost their natural shape. Garhwali women usually invest their savings in silver and gold ornaments—nose-rings, earrings, bangles and bracelets, and sometimes necklaces of old silver rupees. At the time of marriage, it is usually the boy's parents who make a gift of land to the parents of an attractive girl, a sort of dowry system in reverse.

This boy's father is a corporal in the Army and is away for most of the year. When Gajadhar marries, his wife will most likely stay in the village with his mother to help look after the fields, house, goats and buffalo. Gajadhar will see her only when he comes home on leave.

The village is far above the river and most of the fields depend on rainfall. But water must be fetched for cooking, washing and drinking. So, after a breakfast of hot milk and thick chapattis stuffed with minced radish, the brother and I set off down the rough track to the river.

The sun has climbed the mountains, but it has yet to reach the narrow valley. We bathe in the river, the brothers diving in off a massive rock; but I wade in circumspectly, unfamiliar with the river's depths and currents. The water, a milky blue, has come from the melting snows and is very cold. I bathe quickly and then make a dash for a strip of sand where a little sunshine has split down the hillside in warm, golden pools of light. At the same time the song of the whistling-thrush emerges like a dark secret from the wooded shadows.

The Manjari school is only up to class five and has about forty pupils. And if these children (mostly boys) would like to continue their schooling, then, like Chakradhar, they must walk the five miles to the high school in the next big village.

'Don't you get tired walking ten miles every day?' I asked him.

'I am used to it,' says Chakradhar. 'And I like walking.'

I know that he has only two meals a day—one at seven in the morning when he leaves home, and the other at six or seven in the evening when he returns from school. I ask him if he gets hungry on the way.

'There is always some wild fruit,' he says.

He is an expert on wild fruit: the purple berries of the thorny kingora (barberry) ripening in May and June; wild strawberries like drops of blood on the dark green monsoon grass; sour cherries, wild pears and raspberries. Chakradhar's strong teeth and probing tongue extract whatever tang or sweetness lies hidden in them. In the spring there are the rhododendron flowers. His mother makes them into jam, but Chakradhar likes them as they are. He places the petals on his tongue and chews till the sweet juice trickles down his throat. He has never been ill.

'But what happens when someone is ill?' I ask, knowing that in the village there are no medicines, no hospital.

'He rests until he feels better.' says Gajadhar. 'We have a few remedies. But if someone is very sick, we carry him to the hospital at Lansdowne.'

Fortunately the clear mountain air and simple diet keep the people of this area free from most illness. The greatest dangers come from unexpected disasters, such as an accident with an axe or scythe or an attack by a wild animal such as a bear.

I am woken one night by a rumbling and thumping on the roof. I wake Gajadhar and ask him what is happening.

'It's only a bear,' he says.

'Is it trying to get in?'

'No. It's been in the cornfield and now it's after the pumpkins on the roof.'

At the approach of winter, when snow covers the higher mountains, the brown and black Himalayan bears descend to lower altitudes in search of food. Being short-sighted and suspicious of anything that moves, they can be dangerous; but like most wild animals they avoid humans when they can and are aggressive only when accompanied by their cubs.

Gajadhar advises me to run downhill if chased by a bear.

Bears, he says, find it easier to run uphill than downhill!

The idea of being chased by a bear does not appeal to me, but the following night I stay up with him to try and prevent the bear from depleting his cornfield. We take up our position on a high promontory of rock, which gives us a clear view of the moonlit field.

A little after midnight, the bear comes down to the edge of the field. Standing up as high as possible on his hind legs, and peering about to see if the field is empty, he comes cautiously out of the forest and makes his way towards the corn.

Suddenly he stops, his attention caught by some Buddhist prayer-flags which have been strung up recently by a band of wandering Tibetans. Noticing the flags, he gives a little grunt of disapproval and begins to move back into the forest. But then, being one of the most inquisitive animals, he advances again and stands on his hind legs looking at the flags, first at one side and then at the other.

Finding that the flags do not attack him, the bear moves confidently up to them and tears them all down.

After making a careful examination of the flags, he moves into the field.

This is when Gajadhar starts shouting. The rest of the village wakes up and people come out of their houses beating drums and empty kerosene-oil tins.

Deprived of his dinner, the bear takes off in a bad temper. He runs downhill, and at a good speed too; and I am glad that I am not in his way just then. Uphill or downhill, an angry bear is best given a very wide berth.

For Gajadhar, impatient to know the result of his army entrance exam, the following day is a test of patience.

The postman has yet to arrive. The mail is brought in relays from Lansdowne, and the Manjari postman, who has to deliver letters at several small villages enroute, should arrive around noon, but now it is three in the afternoon.

First we hear that there has been a landslide and that the postman cannot reach us. Then we hear that although there had been a landslide, the postman passed the spot in safety. Another alarming rumour has it that the postman disappeared with the landslide. This is soon denied. The postman is safe. It is only the mailbag that has disappeared.

Anyway, he is soon forgiven (and given another heavy meal), because Gajadhar has passed his exam and will leave with me in the morning.

His mother insists on celebrating her son's success by feasting her friends and neighbour. There is a partridge (a present from a neighbour who conjectures that Gajadhar will make a fine husband for his daughter), and three chickens: rich fare for folk whose normal diet consists mostly of lentils, rice, potatoes and onions.

After dinner there are songs, and Gajadhar's mother sings of the homesickness of those who are separated from their loved ones and their homes in the hills. It is an old Garhwali folk song:

Oh mountain swift, you are from my father's home—
Speak, oh speak, in the courtyard of my parents,
My mother will hear you.
She will send my brother to fetch me.
A grain of rice alone in the cooking-pot
Cries, 'I wish I could get out!'
Likewise I wonder—
Will I ever reach my father's house?

The hookah is passed round, and stories are told, gossip

exchanged. It is almost midnight when the last guest leaves. Chakradhar approaches me as I am about to retire for the night.

'Will you come again?' he asks.

'I'm sure I will,' I reply. 'If not next year, then the year after.'

The moon has not yet come up. Lanterns swing in the dark. Almost everyone, including the blind man, carries a lantern. And if you ask the blind man what he needs a lantern for, he will reply: 'So that fools do not stumble against me in the dark.'

The lanterns flit silently over the hillside and go out one by one. This Garhwali day, which is just like any other day in the hills, slips quietly into the silence of the mountains.

I stretch myself out on my cot. Outside the small window, the sky is brilliant with stars. As I close my eyes, someone brushes against the lime tree, bruising its leaves; and the good fresh fragrance comes to me on the night air, making the moment memorable for all time.

THE DEHRA I KNOW

Formally, it's now known as Dehra Dun, but in the 1940s and '50s, when we were young, everyone called it Dehra.

That's where I spent much of my childhood, boyhood, and early manhood, and it was the Dehra I wrote about in many of my books and stories.

It was very different from the Dehra Dun of today—much smaller, much greener, considerably less crowded; sleepier too, and somewhat laid-back, easy-going; fond of gossip, but tolerant of human foibles. A place of bicycles and pony-drawn tongas. Only a few cars; no three-wheelers. And you could walk almost anywhere, at any time of the year, night or day.

The Dehra I knew really fell into three periods. The Dehra of my childhood, staying in my grandmother's house on the Old Survey Road (not much left of that bungalow now). The Dehra of my schooldays, when I would come home for the holidays to stay with my mother and stepfather—a different house on almost every visit, right up until the time I left for England. And then the Dehra of my return to India, when I lived on my own in a small flat above Astley Hall and wrote many of my best stories.

While I was in England, I wrote my first novel *The Room on the Roof*, which was all about the Dehra I had left and the people and young friends I had known and loved. It was a little immature, but it came straight from the heart—the heart and mind of a seventeen-year-old—and if it's still fresh today, fifty years after its first publication, it's probably because it was so spontaneous and unsophisticated.

Back in Dehra, I wrote a sequel of sorts, *Vagrants in the Valley*. It wasn't as good, probably because I had exhausted my adolescence as a subject for fiction; but it did capture aspects of life in Dehra and the Doon valley in the early '50s.

I had returned to India and Dehra when I was twenty-one, and set up my writing shop, so to speak, in that flat above Bibiji's provision store.

Bibiji was my stepfather's first wife. He and my mother had moved to Delhi, leaving Bibiji with the provision store. I got on very well with her and helped her with her accounts, and she gave me the use of her rooms above the shop. I think it's only in India that you could find such a situation—a young offspring of the Raj, somewhat at odds with his mother and Indian stepfather, choosing to live with the latter's abandoned first wife!

Bibiji made excellent parathas, shalgam (turnip) pickle, and kanji, a spicy carrot juice. And so, romantic though I may have been, I was far from being the young poet starving in a garret, nor was Bibiji to be pitied. She was Dehra's first woman shopkeeper, and she managed very well.

Bibiji was of course much older than me; heavily built, strong. She could toss sacks of flour about the shop. Her son, rather mischievous, kept out of her reach; a cuff about the ears would send him sprawling. She suffered from a hernia, and was immensely grateful to me for bringing her a hernia-belt from England; it provided her with considerable relief.

I was quite happy cooking up stories, most of them written after dark by the light of a kerosene lantern. Bibiji hadn't been able to pay the flat's accumulated electricity bills, and as a result the connection had been cut. But this did not bother me. I was quite content to live by candlelight or lamplight. It lent a romantic glow to my writing life.

And a lot of romance went into those early stories. There was the girl on the train in 'The Eyes Are Not Here', and the girl selling baskets on the platform at Deoli, and Aunt Mariam's amours behind the Dilaram Bazaar, and romantic episodes in places as unlikely as Shamli and Bijnor (Pipalnagar). However, as my intention is to give the reader a picture of Dehra as I knew it, the stories in this collection are all set in Dehra Dun and its immediate environs. I was writing for anyone who would read me. It was only much later that I began writing for children.

Some favourite places for my fictional milieu were the parade-ground or maidaan, the Paltan Bazaar and its offshoots, the lichee gardens of Dalanwala, the tea-gardens, the quiet upper reaches of the Rajpur Road (non-transformed into shopping malls), the sal forests near Rajpur, the approach to Dehra by road or rail, and of course the railway station which is much the same as it used to be.

When I was a boy, many of the bungalows (such as the one built by my grandfather) had fairly large grounds or compounds—flower gardens in front, orchards at the back. Apart from lichees, the common fruit trees were papaya, guava, mango, lemon, and the pomalo, a sort of grapefruit. Most of those large compounds have now been converted into housing-estates. Dehra's population has gone from fifty thousand in 1950 to over seven lakh at present. Not much room left for fruit trees!

Some of the stories, such as 'A Handful of Nuts' and 'Living Without Money', were written long after I'd left Dehra, but I think the atmosphere of the place comes through quite strongly in them. When a writer looks back at a particular place or period in his life, he tries to capture the essence of the place and the experience.

During the two years I freelanced from Bibiji's flat (1956–58), I produced over thirty short stories, a couple of novellas, and numerous articles of an ephemeral nature. I managed to sell some of the stories to the BBC's Home service programme— *The Thief, Night Train at Deoli, The Woman on Platform 8, The Kitimaber*—others to the *Elizabethan, Illustrated Weekly of India, Sunday Statesman* (over the years, a few have been lost.) In India, ₹50 was the most you got for a short story or article back then, but you could live quite comfortably on three or four hundred rupees a month—provided your mode of transport was limited to the bicycle. Only successful businessmen and doctors owned cars.

My stepfather was an exception. He was an unsuccessful businessman who used a different car every month. That was because, before leaving Dehra, he ran a motor workshop, and if a car was left with him for repairs or overhauling ('oiling and greasing' he called it) he would use it for a month or two on the pretext of trying it out, before returning it to its owner. This he would do only when the owner's patience had reached its limit; sometimes the car had to be taken away by force. Occasionally, my stepfather would relent and return the car of his own accord—along with a bill for having looked after it for so long!

His talents went unappreciated in Dehra. When he moved to Delhi he became a successful salesperson.

Some of the characters in my Dehra stories were fictional, some were based on real people; Granny was real, of course. And so were the boys in 'The Room' and 'Vagrants'. But did Rusty really make love to Meena Kapoor? It's a question I have often been asked and must leave unanswered. It might have happened. But then again, it might not. I prefer to leave it as a sweet mystery that will never be solved.

One thing is certain. Dehra played an integral part in my development as a writer. More than Shimla, where I did my schooling. More than London, where I lived for nearly four years. More than Delhi, where I spent a number of years. As much as Mussoorie, where I have passed half my life. It must have been the ambience of the place, something about it, that suited my temperament.

But it's a different place now, and no longer do I feel like 'singin' in the rain' as I walk down the Rajpur Road. I am in danger of being knocked down by a speeding vehicle if I try out my old song-and-dance routine. So I keep well to the side of the pavement and look out for known landmarks—an old peepal tree, a familiar corner, a surviving bungalow, a bookshop, the sabzi-mandi, a bit of wasteland where once we played cricket.

There was a wild flower, a weed, that grew all over Dehra and still does. We called it Blue Mint. It grows in ditches, in neglected gardens, anywhere there's a bit of open land. It's there nearly all the year round. I've always associated it with Dehra. The burgeoning human population has been unable to suppress it. This is one plant that will never go extinct. It refuses to go away. I have known it since I was a boy, and as long as it's there I shall know that a part of me still lives in Dehra.

THE GENTLE NIGHTS BEFRIEND ME

Here in Landour, India, on the first range of the Himalayas, I have grown accustomed to the night's brightness—moonlight, starlight, lamplight, firelight! Even fireflies and glow-worms light up the darkness.

Over the years, the night has become my friend. On the one hand, it gives me privacy; on the other, it provides me with limitless freedom.

Not many people relish the dark. Some even sleep with their lights burning all night. They feel safer with the lights on. Safer from the phantoms conjured up by their imaginations.

And yet, I have always felt safer by night, provided I do not deliberately wander about on cliff-tops or roads where danger may lurk. It's true that burglars and other lawbreakers often work by night. They are not into communing with the stars. Nor are late-night revelers, who are usually to be found in brightly lit places and so are easily avoided.

I feel safer by night, yes, but then I have the advantage of living in the mountains, in a region where crime is comparatively rare. I know that if I were living in a big city in some other part of the world, I would think twice about walking home at midnight, no matter how pleasing the night sky.

Walking home at midnight in Landour can be quite eventful, but in a different way. One is conscious all the time of the silent life in the surrounding trees and bushes. I have smelled a leopard without seeing it. I have seen jackals on the prowl. I have watched foxes dance in the moonlight. I have seen flying squirrels flit from one treetop to another. I have observed pine martens on their nocturnal journeys, and listened to the calls of nightjars, owls and other birds who live by night.

Not all on the same night, of course. That would be too many riches at once. Some night walks are uneventful. But usually there is something to see or hear or sense. Like those foxes dancing in the moonlight.

Who else, apart from foxes, flying squirrels and night-loving writers, are at home in the dark?

The nightjars, for one. They aren't much to look at, although their large, lustrous eyes gleam uncannily in the light of a lamp. But their sounds are distinctive. The breeding call of the Indian nightjar resembles the sound of a stone skimming over the surface of a frozen pond; it can be heard for a considerable distance.

Another nightjar species utters a loud grating call which, when close at hand, sounds exactly like a whiplash cutting the air. Horsfield's nightjar (with which I am more familiar) makes a noise similar to that made by striking a plank with a hammer.

I must not forget the owls, those most celebrated of night birds, much maligned by those who fear the night.

Most owls have very pleasant calls. The little jungle owlet has a note that is both mellow and musical. One misguided writer has likened its call to a motorcycle starting up, but this is libel. If only motorcycles sounded like the jungle owl, the world would be a more peaceful place in which to live and sleep.

The little Scops owl speaks only in monosyllables, occasionally saying 'wow' softly, but with great deliberation. He will continue to say 'wow' at intervals of about a minute for hours throughout the night.

Probably the most familiar of Indian owls is the spotted owlet—a noisy bird that pours forth a volley of chuckles and squeaks in the early evening and at intervals all night. Toward sunset, I watch the owlets emerge from their holes, one after another. Before they come out, they stick out their queer little round heads with staring eyes. After emerging, they usually sit very quietly for a time as though only half awake. Then, all of a sudden, they begin to chuckle, finally breaking into a torrent of chattering. Having apparently 'psyched' themselves into the right frame of mind, they spread their short, rounded wings and sail off for the night's hunting.

I wend my way homeward. 'Night with her train of stars' is enticing. The English poet W.E. Henley found her so. But he also wrote of 'her great gift of sleep', and it is this gift that I am about to accept with gratitude and humility. For it is also good to be up and dancing in the morning dew.

ONCE YOU HAVE LIVED WITH MOUNTAINS

It was while I was living in England in the jostle and drizzle of London, that I remembered the Himalayas at their most vivid. I had grown up amongst those great blue and brown mountains, they had nourished my blood, and though I was separated from them by thousands of miles of ocean, plain and desert, I could not forget them. It is always the same with mountains. Once you have lived with them for any length of time, you belong to them. There is no escape.

And so, in London in March, the fog became a mountain mist and the boom of traffic became the boom of the Ganges emerging from the foothills. I remembered a little mountain path which led my restless feet into a cool sweet forest of oak and rhododendron and then on to the windswept crest of a naked hilltop. The hill was called Cloud's End. It commanded a view of the plains on one side, and of the snow peaks on the other. Little silver rivers twisted across the valley below, where the rice fields formed a patchwork of emerald green. And on the hill itself the wind made a 'hoo-hoo-hoo' in the branches of the tall deodars where it found itself trapped. During the rains, clouds enveloped the valley but left the hills alone, an island in the sky. Wild sorrel grew among the rocks, and there were many flowers—convolvulus, clover, wild begonia, dandelion—sprinkling the hillside.

On a spur of the hill stood the ruins of an old building, the roof of which had long since disappeared and the rain had beaten the stone floors smooth and yellow. Moss, ferns and Maidenhair grew from the walls. In a hollow beneath a flight of worn stone steps a wild cat had made its home. It was a beautiful grey creature, black-striped with pale great eyes. Sometimes it watched me from the steps or the wall, but it never came near.

No one lived on the hill, except occasionally a coal-burner in a temporary grass thatched hut. But villagers used the path for grazing their sheep and cattle on the grassy slopes. Each cow or sheep had a bell suspended from its neck to let the shepherd boy know its whereabouts.

The boy could then lie in the sun and eat wild strawberries without fear of losing his animals. I remembered some of the shepherd boys and girls. There was a boy who played the flute. Its rough, sweet, straightforward notes travelled clearly through the mountain air. He would greet me with a nod of his head, without taking the flute from his lips.

There was a girl who was nearly always cutting grass for fodder. She wore heavy bangles on her feet and long silver earrings. She did not speak much either, but she always had a wide smile on her face when she met me on the path. She used to sing to herself, or to the sheep, or to the grass, or to the sickle in her hand. And there was a boy who carried milk into town (a distance of about five miles) who would often fall into step with me to hold a long conversation. He had never been away from the hills or in a large city. He had never been on a train.

I told him about the cities and he told me about his village, how they made bread from maize, how fish were to be caught in the mountain streams, how the bears came to steal his father's pumpkins. Whenever the pumpkins were ripe, he told me, the bears would come and carry them off. These things I remembered—these, and the smell of pine needles, the silver of oak leaves and the red of maple, the call of the Himalayan cuckoo, and the mist, like a wet face-cloth, pressing against the hills.

Odd, how some little incident, some snatch of conversation comes back to one again and again in the most unlikely places. Standing in the aisle of a crowded tube train on a Monday morning, my nose tucked into the back page of someone else's newspaper, I suddenly had a vision of a bear making off with a ripe pumpkin! A bear and a pumpkin—and there, between Belsize Park and the Tottenham Court Road station, all the smells and sounds of the Himalayas came rushing back to me.